W9-DES-185

Praise for *Northanger Alibi*

"*Northanger Alibi* reminds us in comical, relatable ways that mythical creatures aren't always what they're cracked up to be, and that real boys can be even better." —Eve'sFanGarden.com

"*Northanger Alibi* will have you laughing out loud at Claire's observations and dramatic responses. In a world where every teen girl is looking for her 'Edward' . . . , Claire's coming-of-age story is both timely and refreshing." —Amanda Washington, author of *Rescuing Liberty*

"*Northanger Alibi* by Jenni James is one of the best new young adult books of the year. Bringing together the lost beauty and drama of Jane Austen's novels with the hip teen culture of today. Absolutely wonderful and addictive." —Brynna Curry, author of *Earth Enchanted*

"I fell in love with Claire and Tony the same way I fell in love with Edward and Bella in *Twilight. Northanger Alibi* has all the ingredients of a great love story." —Greta Gunselman, killerromance.com

"Northanger Alibi was incredibly adorable and delightfully entertaining. Claire Hart is an exact replica of the standard crazy and young *Twilight* fan; gullible, obsessed and in love with the idea of vampires and werewolves actually being real. . . . Mixing humor, romance and the ultimate crazy *Twilight* fan antics, this book will have you giggling from start to finish!" —Katie

"Stephenie Meyer meets Jane Austen in this humorous, romantic tale of a girl on a mission to find her very own Edward

Cullen. I didn't want it to end!" —Mandy Hubbard, author of *Prada & Prejudice*

"It is a laugh-out-loud book! You will fall in love with Claire and everything that goes with her. . . . I am glad that someone has taken my beloved *Northanger Abbey* and modernized it. . . . *Northanger Alibi* is fun, exciting, and suspenseful. . . . James has hit the nail on the head with this one!" —Keyth A. Pankau

"I found myself laughing out loud . . . and then crying with Claire through her struggles. Yes, it is for young adults . . . but as an adult I completely enjoyed myself too! . . . I love that it is "clean" and there is nothing that I felt like I wouldn't want my daughter to read someday. . . . Trust me, young and old alike won't be disappointed!" —Kari

"[Northanger Alibi] is a laugh-out-loud kinda book! . . . You won't be able to stop the pages from turning!" —Tiffany

"This a is fun, smart, funny story. . . . I couldn't put it down . . . I loved the characters. I loved the story. In short, I just plain loved this book!!" —Candi

"A very funny, very modern remake of Jane Austen's *Northanger Abbey.* I LOVED it!" —Laura

Praise for *Pride & Popularity* by Jenni James

"This book was unputdownable. I highly recommend it to any fan of Jane Austen, young or old." —Jenny Ellis, Jane Austen Society of North America

"This was an absolutely captivating read from the very first page. . . . I bought into every twist and turn and couldn't wait for Taylor and Chloe to actually get it together enough to become a couple." —Shanti Krishnamurty, author of *Maid of Sherwood*

"One of the best remakes of *Pride and Prejudice* ever!" —Jinx

"This is so flippin' cute." —Sweetly Southern

"Pride & Popularity is freaking A-MAZ-ING!" —im-reading-here

"I just absolutely love this story!! Eeep!! <3 <3 <3" —Rachiee

"This was the best book I've ever read on [Wattpad]!!! So freaking good. And what was really cute is that it was sort of innocent and not like a trashy they-sleep-with-each-other-every-other-chapter kinda book." —Christyfanning

"Pride & Popularity is the perfect guilty pleasure read." —Ranee

"If you love Jane Austen's works, YA books, or if you just love a good book, *Pride & Popularity* is a must read!" —Shermia

"This was a fun book full of whit and charm." —Lori

"Definitely a story that will remain at the top of your bookshelf forever!" —FleurRebelle9797

"[Jenni James's] modern spin has you falling in love with a cocky, arrogant Taylor Anderson and a strong willed, outspoken Chloe Hart. This book will make you laugh, cry, scream and smile. If Miss Austen was with us today she would be proud of this book." —Savetheoutcasts

"*Pride & Popularity* is a delightful romantic comedy that will tug on the heartstrings of ladies—regardless of their age. . . . The fast-paced storyline will draw you in while the characters enchant you. . . . If you're looking for a refreshing reminder of how young, innocent love can break through even the most prideful of prejudices, you don't want to miss this one." —Amanda Washington, author of *Chronicles of the Broken*

"A delightful read! A book any *Pride and Prejudice* lover will be unable to put down!" —Jakki

"Having read several other Young Adult retellings of *Pride and Prejudice* . . . I must admit that *Pride & Popularity* by Jenni James is my top choice and receives my highest recommendation! In my opinion, it is the most plausible, accessible, and well-crafted YA version of *Pride and Prejudice* I have read!" —Meredith, Austenesque Reviews

The Jane Austen Diaries

Pride & Popularity
Northanger Alibi
Persuaded (Spring 2012)
Emmalee (Fall 2012)
Mansfield Ranch (Spring 2013)
Sensible & Sensational (Fall 2013)

The Jane Austen Diaries

NORTHANGER ALIBI

JENNI JAMES

This is a work of fiction, and the views expressed herein are the sole responsibility of the author. Likewise, characters, places, and incidents are either the product of the author's imagination or are represented fictitiously, and any resemblance to actual persons, living or dead, or actual events or locales, is entirely coincidental.

Inkberry Press, LLC
110 South 800 West
Brigham City, Utah 84302

ISBN: 978-0-9838293-1-7

This book is dedicated to my yummy vampire husband, because I believe every girl should have her very own vampire. Trust me on this.

ACKNOWLEDGEMENTS

I would like to thank my Heavenly Father for all the doors he has opened to me on my road to publication, including giving me the patience and determination I needed to learn how to write a book.

Thanks to my family, because they bring me so much happiness and joy. I truly don't know where I would be without them.

And thanks to my Writing Challenge girls, who are my inspiration.

ONE
♥
DREAM COME TRUE

"Are you kidding?" I gasped as I bounced on my family's multicolored striped couch. "You want to take me? Me? To Seattle? Are you sure?"

"Yep." The older woman across from me grinned. "That is, if your parents say you can go." She smiled the sweetest smile I'd ever seen toward my mom and dad, who were perched nervously on the matching loveseat.

"Please, Mom?"

I couldn't believe one of my mom's best friends had just asked me to go with her and her husband on his business trip this summer—to Seattle, of all places! Seattle was only my favorite dreamiest vacation spot ever.

"You really want Claire to come with you?" Mom asked Darlene, clearly hedging. Mom had that deer-in-the-headlights look on her face—you know, the one that reads, "Dang. Now what am I going to do?" She knew Washington was my favorite state and that I would totally give my right arm to go. I had only whined and pleaded every day for the last three years for my parents to take us on a road trip up there.

My mom's problem was letting her baby go. And why she still considered me her baby, I'll never know.

"Are you sure you wouldn't be happier taking Cassidy?" she asked.

Cass? Are you kidding me? "Mo–om." *What planet of Totally Unfair did she come from, anyway?*

Darlene shook her head. "Actually, I was really hoping for a younger girl, since the president of Seattle's Northwest Academy—where most of the meetings will be held—has a couple of children in high school. Cassidy is older than that, right? I promised them the next time I came, I'd bring children their age."

Two things in that little speech stuck out at me—two things I'm sure were meant to excite me but that somehow dampened my whole outlook on the trip: "children" and "promised to bring children."

Great. Are the kids so ugly and weird that Darlene has to bring friends with her so they'll have someone to hang out with?

Yeah, that didn't sit well with me. But surprisingly, it seemed to perk Mom up. "Oh, so there'll be another family there with children Claire's age?" she asked. "She'll have friends?"

"Oh, yes," Darlene said. "They will be so grateful to have her there, you have no idea. They are practically desperate for friends."

"D–desperate for f–friends?" *Um, can we say warning flag, anyone? If they're that worried about having friends, maybe this whole going-to-Seattle-thing wasn't the greatest idea after all.*

"And you'll be gone for how long?" Mom really must've

been warming up to the idea.

Darlene shrugged and smiled. "I don't know. It all depends on how quickly Roger can pick up the training he needs. It could take anywhere from three to four weeks all the way up to eleven or twelve weeks. Claire could be in Washington the whole summer."

The whole summer? Never mind the weirdo high-school-age children. I am so *going! A whole summer in Seattle is worth enduring anything—anything at all.*

"Wow! The whole summer?" Mom gasped. "That's a long time. What do you think, Dave?" She turned a bit to study my dad's face, which was a massively good sign. She only asked for his opinion if she wasn't willing to say no herself, and the chances of my dad saying no were slim.

"I think we should let her go." He smiled over at me, and my heart soared. "Who knows when another opportunity like this will come around?"

Yes!

"Did you know Washington is one of the places Claire has always wished she could go?" Dad asked Darlene.

"Really? Isn't this your lucky day then? When I was a girl, I always wanted to visit somewhere exotic, like Hawaii. I'll never forget the moment I learned Roger had arranged our honeymoon there." She leaned back and laughed softly. "Oh, I shrieked and shrieked and danced around the room. My poor fiancé didn't know what to do with me." She glanced back over at my parents. "I'll bring Roger over later. Maybe we'll treat you guys to dinner or something—we'll see. But I promise we'll definitely get together so we can work out the details. I hope you know you can completely trust us."

"Oh, no. I'm not worried, honestly," Mom said. "I would trust you with any of my girls. It's just I'm not used to being away from Claire that long."

Oh, brother. I rolled my eyes and willed myself not to freak out about her extremely overprotective nature. *As if I would ever do anything wrong. We're talking me here, the good daughter.* My mind wandered back a few years to the day my sister Cassidy nearly caused my parents to have heart attacks when she agreed to meet this crazy guy in secret. Thank goodness our older sister Chloe and her boyfriend Taylor found her in time. In that moment, life at the Hart house changed, and my mom has been completely over-the-top protective of us ever since. It's like she never trusts us anymore. Not that I blame her. I mean, we all thought Blake was pretty cool until he tried to disappear with Cassidy. Then we got a bit freaked out. *Why is it that all it takes is one evil person to ruin everything?*

Well, one thing was for sure—Dad's answer really helped Mom warm up to the idea of me going to Seattle, because she said suddenly, "Okay, I'll let Claire go."

"That's wonderful!" Darlene gushed.

"Really?" I nearly fell off my chair. "Are you serious?"

"Yes. But . . ."

I knew I wouldn't get off that easy. "But?"

"I know this may seem rude, Darlene, but I would feel much better if Cassidy came too."

Okay, yeah, that is rude, I thought. *You can't just bring your kids along to hang out with other people when they haven't been invited. What is she thinking?* I was about to die of embarrassment until I heard—

"Yes, great. I have no problem taking Cassidy too, especially if it means we get to have Claire with us." Darlene was much nicer about it than I expected her to be.

"Thank you! Thank you!" I couldn't help myself—I rushed over and gave Darlene a huge hug. "You're the best!"

"Hey! What are we, chopped liver?" my dad said good-naturedly.

"You know I love you. Thank you." I hugged my parents. "Can I tell Cass, please? I can't wait to see her face."

"Sure, sure." Dad shooed me away. "We need to work out a few minor things with Darlene anyway."

That meant they needed to talk about how much it would cost. I wanted to be long gone when that conversation happened—no reason to feel guilty. "Okay!" I hollered as I skidded down the hall toward Cassidy's room. Then I banged on the door. "Hey, I've got some news. Hurry up."

I could hear my parents and Mrs. Hadley chuckling behind me as Cassidy opened the door. "What's up?"

"Oh my gosh! You're never going to believe where we're going," I exclaimed as I pushed my older sister back into her room and shut the door with my foot.

She laughed and swatted my hands away. "What do you mean? Are they planning a vacation or something?"

"Something like that."

She put her hands on her hips. "Okay, spill."

It came out in one big gush. "Oh my gosh! You know Darlene? Well, she came here to invite me to go to Seattle with her. Can you believe it? I'm totally dying here. Mom got overprotective and demanded that you come too—which I was seriously mortified about—but it doesn't matter because Darlene said yes! You get to come too, to Washington, for at least three weeks but maybe even the whole summer! How cool is that?"

After my monologue, I was so busy catching my breath that it took me a moment to realize Cassidy wasn't jumping around the room like I thought she'd be. In fact, she looked downright upset about it.

"Hey, are you okay? What's wrong?"

"Do I have to go?" That was the last thing I expected to come from her lips.

"Are you kidding? You mean, 'Do I really get to go,' right?"

"No." Cassidy shook her head. "Do I have to go? Like, will Mom let you go without me?"

"There is something seriously wrong with my ears. I know you're not sounding disturbed by this amazing news. I know it." *Sheesh. What is this world coming to?* "And yes, to answer your question, I think Mom would totally freak out if you didn't come too. It was hard enough for her to let me go as it is." *No thanks to your antics with Blake.*

"Can you keep a secret?" Cassidy asked quietly.

No. I'm the worst at keeping secrets. Everyone knows that. "Um, sure. What is it?"

She frowned and looked nervously around the cluttered room as though she was checking to see if we were alone. With a gulp, she leaned forward and whispered, "Promise me you won't tell anyone, okay? Promise?"

Only people I can absolutely trust. "Promise."

Her eyes were huge. "I'm seeing someone."

Huh? "That's your secret? You're seeing someone?"

She looked perturbed. "Well, yeah. That's a big secret!"

"That you're seeing someone?" I snorted and plopped on her bed. "You're talking about Ethan, right?"

Cassidy's jaw dropped. "How in the—? Where did you—?"

"Chloe told me like a year ago."

"No way."

"Yeah. She told a lot of people. That's way old news."

"What? Did she tell Mom and Dad?"

"Um . . . no." I threw a crumpled T-shirt at her. "Chloe's

not stupid. But I wouldn't be surprised if they already know anyway."

"Are you kidding me?" Cassidy threw herself on the bed next to me, obviously dejected. "Mom and Dad would have total seizures, and you know it."

She's probably right. "Come on, they're not that bad."

"Not that bad?" She flipped around and faced me. "Not that bad? You of all people should know what it's been like living through their 'grounding for life' episode." She fell back on the bed again. "Never mind that Ethan is only one of the nicest guys ever. And so different from Blake Winter, it's a joke. Mom and Dad don't trust me to make my own judgments when it comes to guys. I'm eighteen. Really, you'd think they'd lighten up!"

"Cass, it looks like they are," I pointed out. "If this vacation is anything to go by, they trust you a lot."

"Yeah, some trust—banning me from the one guy I have ever really loved for a whole summer."

"A guy they technically don't know exists." *Good grief. Maybe I don't want her to go if she's going to be a major mess.* "Think of it this way, Cassidy. If you manage to bring me back in one piece and prove to them that you're responsible, you could probably very easily include Ethan in the picture once you got home."

She sat up. The imaginary lightbulb above her head flickered and then lit up. "I think you're right." She jumped off the bed and walked over to her window. "So, if I go for like a few weeks this summer, by the time I get back everything will be a whole lot better. I mean, they have to trust me, right?" She spun around with a huge smile on her face. "It's brilliant! Like totally mad-scientist perfect. If Mom and Dad trust me enough to babysit you all the way in Washington, then they'll have to trust me with everything else. Hee hee hee!"

Now she was dancing around the room.

"Come on!" She giggled. "We've only got what, three weeks until summer break? We've got to figure out what to pack!"

Needless to say, I left my older sister much happier than when I'd gone into her room thirty minutes earlier. We planned everything, down to our party clothes, just in case we were lucky enough to go out somewhere. All in all, I was pretty pleased with the idea of going with my sister. She was a lot of fun, if you knew her. Some people only saw her quiet side—the person she'd been ever since the Blake incident—but for a few minutes there, I got a glimpse of the old Cassidy, the Cassidy that probably only Ethan saw these days.

Hmm. Maybe this trip will be better all the way around for a lot of reasons.

I softly closed my door and took a minute to just look around my bedroom. I'd turned sixteen earlier in the year, and I was now almost sixteen and a half. In the pre-Blake days, it would have been the perfect age, because it would have been the time when I could go on my first date. But because of Blake, Dad had threatened to make us wait until we were thirty. Okay, to be fair, I'm sure he would've relented and let me go on a date now if a guy actually asked me.

Yep. That was my sorry state of life. Sixteen, never been on a date, never been kissed, never held hands with a guy, never—well, never *anything*. Totally pathetic, right? I blame it mostly on my randomly weird parents—and the fact that after Chloe and Cassidy were born, there wasn't much magic left in the beauty wand for me.

Don't get me wrong. I'm pretty enough—just not knockout

gorgeous pretty. Take my sisters, for instance. Chloe is a stunning redhead with long, perfectly placed ringlets, who's practically engaged to the hottest guy in Farmington, New Mexico. And Cassidy has the same exact ringlets, just with bright blonde hair and a reputation for being either a massive wild-child flirt—thanks to Blake—or a soft-spoken mouse—again, thanks to Blake.

Anyway, how can you compete against a blonde and a redhead? Especially when I'm not sure what color my completely straight hair is. Sometimes people tell me it looks dirty blonde, and sometimes I've been told it looks brownish.

Fine. So there you have it. I'm the baby in a family of three girls, and my total existence has revolved around the consequences of my older sisters' action.

With a sigh, I walked around my room almost as though I was seeing it for the first time. The feeling was pretty surreal, as if it knew I was about to leave and have an amazing adventure. *Washington!* Just thinking about it made me giggle again. I ran over to my desk, plunked down in the seat, and pulled down the book above me before my brain had even processed what I was doing.

Twilight, the most perfect book in the whole world, and subsequently, my favorite in the series. Carefully, I opened up the well-used paperback and allowed the pages to float down in a happy fan. I could feel the gentle breeze they made against my arm before they nestled down again. Almost by instinct, I thumbed through a couple of worn pages and found my favorite passage. It was, hands down, the most romantic paragraph ever written. I sighed as I read the words of Edward Cullen when he tells Bella that she is the most important thing to him now, and how the thought of hurting her has tortured him.

Then I quickly flipped a couple of pages until I came to

the most poignant of all things ever said by Edward. I vividly remembered shaking when I first read his description of his desperate battle within himself to not kill Bella. All he wanted was to get her alone, but the thought of what killing her would do to his family kept him from it. Little did I know until that moment how much danger she'd been in! Edward wanted to kill her and had thought of ways to do it.

Bella Swan. The most amazing heroine ever written. I mean, what other female character had ever been so easy to relate to, or so perfectly complex and lifelike? There couldn't be another heroine more wonderful than Bella—I was sure of it.

So there it was. My deep, dark secret, the reason behind my fascination with Washington. I was in love with Edward Cullen. And Edward lived in Washington. Plain and simple. According to Stephenie Meyer, Washington has the most rainfall of any state. And as everyone knows, vampires have to live in cloudy places.

Since the Twilight series, I had become rather addicted to and obsessed with all things pertaining to the world of Edward Cullen and Bella Swan. There was so much to learn. The funny thing was, every time I read one of the books, I found something new—something I'd missed before.

And then it hit me.

I'm going to Washington.

I'm really, really, really going.

Honestly, can life get any better than this?

TWO ♥ SEATTLE OR BUST!

Three and a half weeks later, I asked myself the same question repeatedly: *Can life get any better than this?* I thought as I collected my luggage and took it down to the car. I thought it as I hugged and kissed my mom and dad goodbye, promising to say my prayers every night. *Yeah. Say my prayers that I meet Edward.* And then I asked it out loud as we boarded the plane.

By the time we landed, I was in that complete nervous-slash-excited state of mind you get when you're ready for your amazing adventure to begin. I didn't realize how excited I was until I noticed I was practically running down the long ramp to get to the terminal.

Cassidy finally caught up. "Why are you walking so fast, girl? The place isn't on fire!" She panted next to me as she tried to match my long strides.

"Not yet, it isn't. If you give me a couple of minutes, I'm sure I can cause enough friction with these shoes to start a fire."

She giggled. "The way you were moving, I don't doubt it."

Cassidy and I walked out into the open terminal, then stepped aside and stood near a pillar to wait for Roger and Darlene. I felt a momentary stab of guilt when I realized my actions could've been considered rude, running ahead of the group like that. But all my fears were soon put to rest when the Hadleys came bounding down the ramp.

"Well, there they are!" Darlene exclaimed loud enough to be heard by everyone around us. "I'm so glad to see such eagerness. You girls are going to keep me on my toes, I can tell. It's about time, too." She walked over and put an arm through each of ours, and we all followed Roger as he carried their carry-on luggage.

After a happy squeeze and a giggle, Darlene asked, "So, are you two ready for your first real adventure?"

"Yes!" Cassidy and I chorused back, laughing. I had never been more ready for anything in my entire life.

Move over, Seattle. Claire Hart just landed, and I plan on taking you by storm!

So, my storm had to be patient as we unpacked and moved into the small cottage Roger had rented for the summer. Cassidy and I shared a pretty yellow room with two twin beds. There was a tiny closet tucked into the corner, and a long, white French-style dresser for our clothes. Each bed had a charming little white nightstand that matched the dresser, with a cute reading lamp and a personal alarm clock. I chose the bed closest to the window.

Cassidy opened a narrow door she'd found once she closed our bedroom door. She gasped. "What's this?"

Probably another closet, I thought. Unconcerned, I dumped my carry-on on the bed and set my wheeled suitcase next to it.

"Claire, you've got to see this," exclaimed Cassidy in a muffled voice. "You're never going to believe it!"

I looked up and couldn't see her anywhere. The small door was wide open. "Cass?"

"In here! Hurry!"

What in the world? I quickly dropped my camera and purse on the bed and went to the door. When I peered inside, my gasp echoed Cassidy's just moments before. "No way. This is amazing." I actually had to blink twice before I fully comprehended what I was seeing. It was the largest, most decadent bathroom I'd ever seen—at least the size of our room, if not bigger. It was beautiful and bright, with shades of cheerful yellow and pink and white bouncing off the walls and the soft, plush rugs beneath our feet.

Just then, Darlene knocked and then peeked into the bathroom. "This place is great, isn't it?"

I was about to go off about the awesomeness of the claw-footed bathtub, but she went on. "So, girls, Roger's classes don't start until Monday, and since it's only Friday, what do you say we do a bit of sightseeing while we're here?"

"Really?" I said. "That would be awesome." Even Cassidy looked excited.

"Roger and I thought we'd ask the president of Northwest Academy and his family to come, too. What do you think?"

The weird kids—the ones that need friends? My smile waned. "Sure, why not?"

"We did promise them we'd bring someone they could meet," Darlene reminded me.

"Who's this? You promised we'd meet someone?" Cassidy asked.

I'd forgotten I hadn't told my sister anything about the loser teenagers. In hidden disgust, I walked past our host and sat on my bed. I'd let Darlene tell my sister the good news. I had all but blocked out the horror of Darlene's explanation when I heard Cassidy's massive intake of breath. With a grin, I caught her panicked look from the doorway just before she smiled happily at our host, obviously trying not to relay any of the warning flags I'm sure were popping up in her head.

I prayed for rain. Like, big-time rain. You know—enough to cancel our sightseeing tour and put off the inevitable meeting as long as possible.

Well, it did sprinkle, but not enough to keep us away from meeting the paragons of awkwardness. In fact, we were soon standing on the slightly damp grass in front of the Space Needle, watching them walk toward us.

All right, I admit it. Anthony and Eleanor Russo weren't that bad. I mean, sure, there was something about them that just didn't sit right, something in their movements or the way they talked. I don't know—it seemed stilted, not natural. Kind of Stepford-y, if you catch my drift. But other than that, I couldn't complain.

One thing was for sure, they were a whole lot cuter than I thought they'd be. Their whole family was this perfect, white-collar, yuppie-type family. They each had beautiful smiles and beautiful eyes and beautiful clothes.

The parents were Ilene and Jonathan. Both of them looked really young, but they must've been in their early forties. And then there was Anthony, who went by Tony, who had just turned seventeen, and Eleanor—Nora—who we later found out was his twin sister.

They were nice, too—almost too nice. I enjoyed talking to Nora the most, because she seemed just a little bit more real than Tony.

"Have you ever been to Seattle before?" she asked as we boarded a large boat with wheels, part of our Ride the Ducks tour.

"No. Does this vehicle really go in the water, too?"

"You've never been on these before, have you?" She smiled at me, then climbed into a row and patted the bench next to her. "You're going to love this tour. It's really nice."

"Nice?" *Crazy, yes, but nice?*

Cassidy and Tony sat down on the bench across the aisle.

"Fun," Nora amended. "It'll be a lot of fun."

Now "fun" I understood. "Cool."

"Just wait. It'll drive us all around Seattle, so you can see everything up and down the streets, and then it'll drive right down a ramp into the ocean. That's why they're called ducks, because they're on land and then the water. They're really nice."

There was that word again—"nice." Something just wasn't right.

Nora's brother leaned across the narrow walkway between the two benches and asked, "You didn't tell Claire about the part where we go all the way under the water, did you?"

Huh? Under the water? I looked out the sides of the duck-slash-boat thing. There were no windows. Just open air, supports, and a roof. The boat would fill up with water in seconds. "Are you kidding?" I asked him.

Tony's eyes moved from Nora's to mine. It was the first time I had made real eye contact with him.

Wow. He's—he's really cute! And, um, close.

Leaning over like he was, Tony was only about a foot from me. "It's just for a couple of seconds. It's not like you'll drown or anything. You did read the brochure, right? It told you to make sure you only brought waterproof stuff on board."

What in the—? I glanced down at the pamphlet in my hand and back up at him, totally thinking he was serious until I saw a playful glimmer flash in his light brown gaze. "Whatever." I rolled my eyes and tried to push him back toward Cassidy. My hand collided with solid steel. At least, that's what his shoulder felt like to me. Not that I had touched a lot of guy's shoulders, but Tony's felt pretty strong. Really strong, actually. Almost *too* strong.

He must've seen my face because he chuckled nervously, then quickly leaned back into his seat.

A few more passengers moved down the aisle between us and broke our eye contact.

"What'd you say to Claire?" Cassidy asked him.

As I sat forward and tried not to think about how strong his shoulder was, I heard Tony murmur something to Cass. A second later she burst into laughter.

Ha ha.

"Don't mind Anthony," Nora whispered. "He's always trying to tease people. You should see the stuff he does to me." She shuddered dramatically.

It was definitely a sign that they were a normal family. Maybe there was hope for them yet.

I didn't have much time to think about them after that, since the boat thingy started up. For the next hour and a half, I lost myself completely to the zany tour. Even the tour guide was hilarious. I couldn't believe it when he had us singing along with him. He made the most boring sights, like regular cafés and businesses, seem exciting. I couldn't wait to explore them after the tour was over.

When we plunked into the water, the energy level, which had been pretty high before, jumped to colossal proportions. It was incredible to see Seattle from the water—it gave the whole city a sort of picturesque quality.

It was then that it hit me. Really, truly hit me. *Oh my gosh. I can't believe I'm here! I'm in Washington! How did I ever get this lucky?*

So, my first full day in Washington wasn't bad. It was wonderful, actually—it didn't turn out anything like what Cassidy and I had imagined. Thank goodness Nora and Tony weren't total far-fetched basket cases. The day could've been pretty bad.

Dinner at the Space Needle turned out to be a way different story. Believe me—I need a whole chapter to tell that one. Who knew Tony would turn out to be so completely different? I mean, honestly, I don't think anyone could've predicted how our day would end. But now that I've had some time to ponder it, I see the signs were there all along. I just hadn't been wise enough to put them together.

THREE
♥
SECRET REVEALED

It all started out innocently enough. We had begun and ended our day at the Space Needle—with a quick run home and a change of clothes, of course. This time we were going inside, and none of us wanted to go to Seattle's coolest restaurant in jeans and T-shirts.

The Space Needle was huge. I didn't think so just by looking at the picture, but when you stand right underneath it, the building is pretty impressive. It's awe inspiring the way that large spaceship-looking thing is balanced on such narrow legs. Whoever designed it must've been a complete genius.

The ride to the top in the elevator was crazy. Even though it took less than a minute, it felt like five.

Cassidy gasped. "My stomach is going to fall right out this window." Everyone in the elevator laughed.

I knew exactly where she was coming from. The farther we climbed—and the more of Seattle we saw below us—the farther my stomach felt from my body. I had no idea I was afraid of heights until that moment.

"Oh, just wait till you get inside," Tony said next to me. "The restaurant spins so you get to see the whole city."

What? "It spins?" I freaked and held on to the side of the elevator. "What do you mean, it spins?"

"Are you kidding?" Cassidy looked green.

Everyone in the elevator laughed again, even the strangers.

"What?" I said.

Nora shook her head and opened her mouth to respond, but Tony was faster. "You can't even tell you're moving, I promise. It rotates so slowly you don't even realize anything has happened until you look out the window and the scenery has changed."

"Well, that's a relief," Cassidy muttered. "For a minute there, I wasn't sure what I had gotten myself into."

I glanced over at Nora to see how she was taking it, but she wasn't paying attention to anyone except Tony. By the looks of things, they had just started a very heated, whispered discussion. Whatever Tony was saying, it wasn't making Nora very happy. *What's going on?*

I tuned out the adults completely to try to hear what Tony and Nora were saying, but the hum of the elevator was so loud I couldn't make out more than a couple of words—"Yeah, well . . ." and "No. Don't even . . ."

My sister was a bit closer to them, and I wondered if she could hear any better. After giving her a nudge with my elbow, I was about to ask if she'd heard anything, when we arrived and the elevator doors opened. *Darn.* Tony and Nora stopped talking and surged forward with everyone else.

"What'd you bump me for?" Cassidy quietly asked as we entered the main lobby of the restaurant.

I leaned toward her but caught Tony's eye. "Nothing, I'll tell you later," I mumbled. Then I exclaimed, "Wow—the food smells awesome. I can't wait to try it."

Mr. Russo walked up to the hostess, and I watched as he slipped a folded bill into her palm and announced our names. She pretended to scan the reservation list, and then said with a smile, "We have your table waiting, sir. If you will please follow me."

I wondered if anyone else noticed Jonathan Russo's bribe. If they did, they didn't say anything or seem to think it was weird. *Huh.* I hitched my purse higher on my shoulder and followed the group, with Cassidy beside me.

"Did you see that?" I whispered.

"See what?" she muttered back.

Glancing behind him, Tony caught my eye again. *The guy must have ears like a jackrabbit.* I smiled. "The flowers on the hostess desk. Weren't they beautiful?"

"Uh, I didn't see them." Cassidy looked at me funny.

I couldn't tell if Tony bought it because he'd already turned around. I didn't know why I was so hesitant to let him hear me, but I was.

Once we got to our table and saw the view of the city from the window, I felt a little lightheaded. It was beautiful, but it was totally weird to be so far above the world and looking down on it, knowing you were basically floating above it all. One side of the rectangular table was against the window, and I chose the opposite side, so I was as far as possible from the window. Unfortunately, so did Tony.

Sheesh. It's like he's trying to keep tabs on me or something.

Nora sat next to him, and Cassidy sat next to me. The adults sat across from each other—women on one side, men on the other. I could tell they were all good friends.

"Are you sure you kids don't want to sit closer to the window?"

Tony's dad asked. "Claire? Cassidy? I'll swap seats with either of you, if you like. The view is much better from here."

"I think it's the view they're trying to avoid, Dad," Tony jumped in.

"Oh, I see." Jonathan smiled knowingly at us before turning his attention to Roger.

Darlene leaned over as the hostess handed Cassidy and me our menus and said, "This is on us. We really want you to enjoy yourselves tonight, so order whatever you want."

"Thanks." I smiled. Then I opened my menu, and the prices of the food hit me full force. *Holy cow!* I gulped. *Forty-five dollars for seafood? Fifty-five dollars for steak? Are you kidding me? That better be one massive piece of meat.* I scanned through the other items to find something more reasonable. I knew the exact second Cassidy became aware of the prices, because she inhaled sharply and then choked out a cough. Her eyes were huge.

I could tell she was doing the same thing I was—trying to find something that didn't cost more than a new pair of mall-quality boots. Fifty dollars could feed our whole family for about three days. Just the thought of spending that much on one meal blew me away.

"What's wrong?"

I looked up to find Tony's eyes resting on me. For a moment I forgot everything else. "What? Oh—uh, nothing."

"Nothing?" He grinned. He really had a nice grin. Like, almost model nice. "Are you sure?"

My heart skipped a beat when I noticed he had a dimple. A really *cute* dimple.

"Claire? Are ya with me?" He smiled again.

My eyes flew to his. I could tell he knew exactly what I was thinking, like he could read my mind. I blushed in humiliation and hid behind my menu. Tony wasn't discouraged.

"Hey." He gently tugged the menu away from me. "Don't cover your face. I like looking at it."

What? My heart stopped. Literally stopped. *Is he serious? There's no way he's serious.* I decided to play it cool and took a breath to get my heart to beat again. "I'm not hiding," my voice squeaked.

Tony's grin deepened, and I noticed another, fainter dimple.

I cleared my throat and tried again. "I—I was wondering what you normally ate when you came here." *There. That wasn't so bad.*

"Me?" His eyes twinkled. "I don't normally eat when I come here."

"You don't normally eat?" I was confused.

"No." He chuckled and folded his menu. "I usually ride the elevator to the top and study the view."

"Oh." *I'm such a dork.* "You don't come to the restaurant?"

"You could say that."

I picked up my menu and scanned it again, trying not to hide behind it this time.

"But I hear the crab cakes are really good. And their seafood trio is awesome. Most people get those together—they're a nice combo."

Nice. There's that word again. I quickly glanced at the two items he mentioned. I gulped again. *Okay, no way.* The combined total was seventy-one dollars. *Sheesh. How did I get roped into coming to this place?* "Thanks." *I decided to stick with soup and salad.* That was only eighteen dollars.

"What are you ordering?" Cassidy asked me under her breath. "I was thinking maybe soup and salad?"

I tried not to giggle. "That's where I was headed."

Our waitress came by and took our order. The Hadleys

wouldn't allow my sister and me to just order starters, no matter how un-hungry we proclaimed ourselves to be. After we placed our orders, they made us choose a meal, too. We both settled on the cheapest thing—roasted chicken.

The soup and salad were so good that by the time the rest of the food came, my mouth was watering. All at once, I didn't care how much was being spent on me. The food was amazing. Cassidy and I both dug in—in a very ladylike way, of course. We were halfway through our meals before I looked up and saw Tony resting his head on his hand, pushing his salmon and prawns around his plate with his fork. It didn't look like he'd eaten any of it.

"Hey, are you going to eat?"

He was so startled by my question, he dropped his fork against the plate. "Oh, you noticed?"

"Yeah." *Was I not supposed to?*

He sat up and smiled a quick, short smile, then looked down at his plate. "Uh, well, I don't think I'm feeling that good, actually."

"Are you sick?" I was worried.

Tony glanced up, looking surprised. He must've realized I was concerned, because he straightened up and collected his fork. "Hey, no worries. I'm all right." He stirred a chunk of salmon around in a thick, creamy sauce before he brought it up to his lips. I didn't miss his slight hesitation before he opened his mouth and swallowed the whole thing without chewing.

Oh my gosh, he is *sick!*

His head snapped up, and he looked right at me. He studied my features intently for a moment before he mumbled, "You know, I think you may be right. I think I *am* sick."

His mom heard him, and she snickered across the table loud enough for everyone to hear. "You? That's impossible." Then, for Darlene's benefit, she loudly whispered, "Anthony has never been ill a day in his life."

Tony's eyes were still focused on me. Looking down, I could feel his stare on the top of my head. It was so weird.

What's he thinking? Why is he staring at me? Look at Cassidy or Nora or the view outside, for crying out loud.

I took another bite of my dinner, but the food had lost its flavor. I washed it down with a gulp of the restaurant's famous spring water.

"Sorry."

I glanced up and saw Tony leaning toward me.

He shifted nervously in his chair, then said again, softly, "Sorry."

"F–for what?" There was something going on here that I didn't understand.

"For staring at you just now. I didn't mean to make you uncomfortable."

Okay, *now* I was uncomfortable. *How perceptive is this guy, anyway?*

"Very," he muttered.

"Excuse me?" I gasped. *Had I said that last thought out loud?*

Tony jerked back like I had slapped him. "Uh—very." He looked around nervously, then shook his head and grimaced. "Look, I'm very sorry, okay? That's all."

Oh, he's very sorry? For a minute there I thought he'd . . . I looked back up. He was staring at me again, watching me intently. His eyes were lighter than any brown eyes I had ever seen before, and they simmered with emotion.

Holy cow.

That's when it hit me—spinning five hundred feet in the Washington sky—and everything clicked into place.

Anthony Russo was a vampire.

FOUR

♥

MY OWN TWILIGHT

"Are you out of your mind?" Cassidy nearly shouted, loud enough to rock the cottage while she paced in our bedroom later that night.

"Shh!" I hissed, instantly regretting that I'd told her about Tony.

"Claire, you can't go around declaring that people have sold their souls to the devil and not have me freaking out! What gave you such a crazy idea, anyway?"

"Vampires are not evil. They don't—"

"They're blood-sucking people who feed off other life forms, mainly humans! Living, breathing humans. How is that not evil?"

She was blowing this way out of proportion. "Look—"

"No, you look. This is ridiculous. You're ridiculous. Oh my gosh!" She whipped around and headed straight for the bed where I sat. "Please tell me you haven't told anyone else about this. Please, please, please tell me I'm the only one who knows you think Tony Russo is a vampire."

I rolled my eyes. *Like I'm that stupid.* "Of course you're the only one who knows. Come on, give me a break."

"Claire. Do you have any idea what type of 'break' this would be for our family if word got out you were accusing the son of the director of Northwest Academy of being a stupid vampire?"

That was it. She'd gone too far. "Vampires are not stupid, Cassidy!" I stood up and glared at her. "And excuse me, but I believe I would know if I met one or not."

She walked over to her bed and collapsed. "Are you kidding me? You actually believe in them? *Them?* As in, you think there are more? Ugh. And I thought this babysitting thing was going to be easy."

"Of course I believe in them. Vampires are real, Cass."

"Why me?" She rolled over on her side and stared at me before she shook her head. "Claire, fine. You win. I'm sure—I'm positive—that there are some pretty sick people in this world. Even sick enough to drink human blood. So in a sense, they're vampires. But if you think for one minute that—"

"But Stephenie Meyer says—"

"Stephenie Meyer? Is that what this is all about?" Cassidy sat up and rolled off the bed. In two seconds, she was rummaging through my side of the dresser.

"Hey!" I ran over to her, but I was too late. She had already found my *Twilight* book. "What are you doing with that?"

"This is a book, Claire. A book. This isn't real." She shook it above her head for emphasis.

I jumped up and tried to get it, but she was taller than me. "I know that. What do you think I am, a baby? Duh. Everyone knows *Twilight* came from a dream." I jumped again and snagged the sleeve of her pajama top, pulling her arm down with it. "Give me my book."

Cassidy sighed and released her hold, letting me take the book from her. "Do you really know it's not real, Claire?"

"Yes." I stomped over to my bed and set the book carefully on the nightstand.

"Then what makes you think Tony's a vampire?" she asked warily as she headed back to her bed.

I sat down and shrugged. "Everything."

"And?"

I crossed my legs. "Okay, did you happen to notice how he knew what I was thinking?"

"Uh, no. I must've missed that."

"Did you feel how strong he was? He felt like steel."

Cassidy's eyebrows shot up. "Wait. You touched Tony's muscles?"

"Yeah. And he's a whole lot stronger than he looks."

"You touched his muscles? When did this happen?"

"On the Ride the Duck tour. Why?"

"Well, where was I?"

"Right next to him."

"Oh." She blinked and then asked, "So this is what makes you think he's a vampire—he's strong? And he knows what you're thinking?"

"And he wouldn't eat his food, because he said he was sick. Except, then his mom said he never gets sick."

"And because he was sick, you concluded that he was a vampire?" I could tell my sister thought I'd totally lost it.

"Yes, because being sick was just an excuse not to eat. Vampires don't like to eat regular food. And . . ." I fiddled with my hands.

"And?"

"And he stared at me a lot."

"Oh my gosh," Cassidy mumbled under her breath. "Are

you for real?"

"Yes, Miss Know-it-all, I am."

Cassidy started to giggle.

"Ha ha. Very funny."

She laughed harder.

"You know I'm going to prove you wrong, right?"

Her laughter turned to snorts. Very stupid-sounding pig snorts, I might add. It wasn't funny. "I *will* prove you wrong!"

She fell off the bed. My sister was literally rolling on the floor laughing. And she thought *I* was the idiot.

"You know, you can stop now," I decided to add after another minute of listening to her hilarity.

"I know!" She gasped. "But—but—b–b–but it's j–j–just soooo fu-nnyyy!"

"Ha ha." I got up off my bed. "You know, knock yourself out, okay? Have a good li'l party down there, thinking all about Tony being a vampire." She burst into more laughter. "I'm gonna go wash this gunk off my face." I pointed to my makeup in case she was watching. She wasn't. With a huge sigh, I stepped over my lunatic sister. Then I walked into the bathroom and slammed the door behind me. Peals of laughter vibrated off the walls, and I willed myself not to roll my eyes again. *I will prove her wrong. Tony Russo is a vampire, and I know it.*

I waited until Cassidy had calmed down completely before I ventured into our room again. She was reading *Twilight,* propped against her pillows and the headboard.

"Hey, that's off limits."

She smirked. "Just brushing up on my vamp knowledge. I'll give it back when you need it."

Like I need it. I practically had the thing memorized. "Don't worry. Go ahead and use it. *You'll* need it."

She snapped the book shut.

Ooh. That got to her.

"So, what are you going to do if he lures you away from everyone else and bites you?" she asked with a smirk.

"I thought you were through."

"So did I!" She giggled and raised her hands in a defensive pose. "Okay, okay. I promise I'll stop now, okay?"

"Promises, promises," I mumbled, then climbed between the sheets and turned off my lamp.

Cassidy's lamp was still on. It illuminated her bed and made her light blonde hair glow like a halo around her head. She set the book on the nightstand, and I watched her climb down to say her prayers.

Sheesh. I totally forgot. Grudgingly, I pushed the covers off and knelt on the floor by the bed. My bare toes wiggled against her sock-covered ones before I started my prayer.

Cassidy had gotten back in bed and turned off her lamp before I'd even finished. I had a lot to thank the Lord for. She would've started laughing again if I gave her a rundown of my silent prayer, so I kept it to myself.

She waited until I was all snuggled in before she asked, "You know what I think it really was?"

"What *what* was?" I asked.

"All those signs with Tony."

"Yeah, what about them?"

"Well . . ." I heard her roll over in her bed to face me. "I've been thinking about it, and I think he likes you."

I turned on my lamp. "What?"

"I'm serious." She smiled. "Why else would a guy let you feel his muscles?"

"He didn't let me feel them. I—"

"And why else would he be watching you all the time?"

He was worried I was onto him?

"Or why else do you think he was too nervous to eat in front of you? So much so, it made him sick."

Now it was my turn to snort. "Whatever, Cass." *Like I've ever made a guy too nervous to eat in front of me.* "Probably because he doesn't prefer to eat food."

She ignored that. "I also think that's why he knew what you were thinking."

"Because he likes me?" *Is she high?*

"Yeah, because he was really into you and watching your reactions and stuff. It let him know what you were thinking."

"Oh, puh-leeze!"

"You are pretty easy to read, you know."

I leaned over and turned off the lamp. "You need to get some more sleep. Obviously, you're still jet-lagged." I sounded calm enough as I said it, but I had to wonder if my heart could still beat properly at the speed it was racing. *Holy cow. Could Cassidy be right? Could Tony be into me? No way.* Just the thought of finding my own Edward nearly drove me over the top. *And to think, it's all happening in Washington!*

The next morning I awoke bright and early, eager to get a start on the day. Despite my crazy dreams and only sleeping half the night, I was amazingly refreshed and full of happy energy. The night before, the Hadleys had mentioned to the Russos that we'd hoped to go to church while we were in town. Our new friends were quick to tell us the direction of their building and the time the service started, so we were all set to go to service with them.

I couldn't wait. It was amazing what twenty-four hours could do to a girl's outlook toward a family. It was like Cassidy and I had done a complete one-eighty. The more I thought about the Russos, the more excited I became.

Once I chose the perfect skirt and top, I headed into the bathroom and primped and curled and beautified myself to perfection. By the time my sister crawled out of bed, I was already downstairs eating a bowl of Grape-Nuts in the kitchen with Roger.

"Hey, sleepyhead," I said after Cassidy groggily acknowledged my presence. "Did you have good dreams?"

"Don't even get me started about the crazy vampire dreams I had last night." She pulled a bowl out of the cupboard and plunked it on the counter.

Roger looked surprised. "Vampires, huh?" he asked around a crunchy mouthful of cereal. "Is that what girls dream about these days?"

"Only certain bloodthirsty-type girls," Cassidy answered, throwing me a withered look.

"Yep." I grinned back. "Cass is about as bloodthirsty as they come."

"Really?" Roger's eyes got wide. "I'll go see how Darlene's getting along, okay?" He glanced at my sister. "We're going to leave in about thirty minutes."

Cassidy gave me a look before she smiled sweetly at Roger. "Don't worry, I'll be ready. I've just got to put on my makeup and get dressed, and I'm good to go."

I could just see the wheels turning in Roger's head as he imagined her showing up at church all Goth. He nodded once, then got out of the kitchen fast.

"The poor guy—I think you scared him," she said as soon as he was out of earshot. "Now he thinks I'm some vampire lover."

I smirked as I put my bowl in the sink. "You sure you don't

want to be? I could ask Tony if he's got a cousin."

"Funny," she murmured as she stepped up to the counter and filled her bowl with cereal. "So, do you still plan on proving to me that Tony's a vampire?"

"Yep." I crossed my arms and leaned against the sink. "How much do you want to bet I'm right?"

"I don't make stupid bets," she answered smugly as she poured the milk. "Besides, I don't need to bet. I know I'm right."

"Fine. How about, if I find out Tony's a vampire—"

"He's not."

"If I find out he is, then you've got to tell Mom and Dad you're going with Ethan."

"What?" She nearly spilled her cereal as she walked over to the kitchen stool.

"Ooh! Are you worried?" I smiled.

"No." She set the bowl down. "Whatever. Then, when you find out I'm right—"

"Which you're not."

"When you find out I'm right, you're going to kiss him."

I gasped. I was glad my bowl was already in the sink, or it would've shattered on the floor when I dropped it. "Are you serious?"

"Worried?" Cassidy smiled around her spoon.

I grinned back. "Bring it on!"

FIVE

MAY THE BEST ~~MAN~~ GIRL WIN!

Tony wasn't at church. His mom said it was because he was sick—which Cassidy was quick to rub in—but I was positive they were just saying that to make his ploy look good.

So, I was bummed, more than I should've been. I hadn't realized quite how excited I was to see him again, or how much my day would be affected when he wasn't there. *Maybe it's love? Hmm.* I didn't know. I wasn't sure how you were supposed to feel when you were in love. But my heart did beat like crazy every time someone mentioned his name—which wasn't enough, in my opinion.

I spent most of the service craning my neck to look behind me. I admit it. It drove Cassidy nuts, too. My mom would've probably given me the evil eye, but nobody else seemed to mind. Part of me hoped that once Tony was all alone in the house, he would get bored and tired of pretending to be sick, and he would come to church anyway. If he was a true vampire, he'd be able to run here so fast, no one could see him.

Oh my gosh! Maybe that's it! Maybe he's already here watching me, like when Edward was watching Bella in the woods. I spun around and sat up straighter, my eyes alert.

"What are you doing?" Cassidy whispered. "Will you pay attention to the sermon, please?"

Now that I thought about it, I *did* feel someone watching me. "Hey, look around. Do you see Tony somewhere?" Just in time, I remembered to whisper.

From the way my sister looked at me, I thought she was going to have a cow. "What? Why would I see Tony?" she asked.

I picked up the hymnal and covered my mouth with it. "Because I feel like someone's watching me."

"Well, duh! You're acting like such a dork, fidgeting around like that, you've probably got the whole congregation watching you."

Yeah, right. I rolled my eyes and banged the hymnal shut. Everyone turned around and looked at me. *Dang.*

"I'm gonna die of embarrassment right now," Cassidy muttered as she scooted farther away from me on the bench. "Could you be a bigger spaz?"

I slid down next to her and raised the hymnal again. "You know what? I don't care what you think," I whispered.

"Claire. Tony Russo is ill, okay? He did not fly with his super bat powers—"

"Run."

"Whatever! He's not here. Okay? And he's definitely *not* watching you."

"How do you know?"

Sometimes Cassidy can make the weirdest gestures, like she's having a seizure or something. Really, I'm not kidding. Downright scary, especially at church, with everyone watching.

She glared at me. "I. Can't. Believe. I'm. Having. This. Conversation."

"Why?"

She whipped her head around and stared at me. "Are you okay? How close did you get to Tony yesterday, anyway?"

Huh?

She put her hand up to my head. "Hmm. You don't feel feverish."

I swatted her away. "Stop it. Of course I'm not sick. Don't you have any imagination at all?"

"Imagina—!"

"Ahem!" Roger interrupted.

We both looked up. Everyone was standing, getting ready to sing. *Ack!* I fumbled with the hymnal, and Cassidy and I scrambled to our feet as quickly as possible. Under the beginning notes of the organ, I explained, "It's obvious he's trying to fake being sick so I won't know he's a vampire."

"Save me, please." She raised her eyes to the vaulted ceiling as everyone began to sing the first verse. "Somebody save me."

"Very funny," I said as I found my place and joined the singing.

"Only you would think so, Claire."

I decided to ignore her for the rest of the meeting. After all, why bother with someone who's just trying to set me up to fail? It was obvious she didn't want to lose the bet.

Three days later, I still hadn't seen Tony again. Roger had started his classes, and Darlene spent most of her days reading blogs and e-mails and keeping up with her online friends. Cassidy and I were basically left to our own devices, and considering the fact that she was still bugging me, it made it very hard being around her. I wasn't bored, exactly—staying in Seattle sure beat staying home. I just wished there was something I could do! Even if Cassidy and I were on friendlier terms, neither of us knew the neighborhood well enough to go very far anyway.

So there we were, twiddling our thumbs for the third day in a row, when thankfully, the doorbell rang. It was Nora. She was alone, but hey, I wasn't complaining.

"I came by to see if you two wanted to go the mall or something."

"Yes!" I beamed like a total idiot. "I love malls. Hold on, let me ask Cass. She's upstairs reading."

"Okay."

"You're welcome to come in and say hi to Darlene," I offered.

"Sure." Nora smiled as she walked through the door.

"She's in the kitchen. I'll be right down," I hollered behind me as I dashed up the stairs. "Cass! Cassidy!" I nearly took the door down in my excitement.

She looked up from reading *Twilight.* I had practically forced her to read the book, figuring that would help me win the bet about Tony. Plus, there was the added fact that it was only the greatest book ever written. And since there wasn't anything else to do, Cassidy had reluctantly agreed. "Yeah?" she said. "What happened?"

For a minute I forgot all about Nora. "Where are you?" I walked over and looked at the page number—54. *Holy cow. This is right where it starts to get really good.*

"Um, I don't know. Let me see . . . she almost cried cuz it seemed like her dad loved her." I noticed Cassidy had her finger saving her spot in the book.

Hee hee hee. She is *getting into it. She doesn't want to lose her place.*

"Was there something you needed?" she asked.

Oh. "Nora came to see if we wanted to go to the mall with her today."

"Uh, the mall?" Cassidy looked torn. She loved the mall. She glanced down at the book, then shook her head. "No, I'd rather just take a break today. You go on without me, and I promise to take a rain check, okay?"

You want to take a break? From what, lying around? Welcome to Twilight, *the most addicting book on the planet.* "Okay, whatever. I'll see ya later." *Enjoy falling for Edward.* I walked over to the door and waved, but she was already reading the book again.

When I made it downstairs, I overheard Darlene talking to Nora.

"Now, take this money. I want you and the girls to go watch a movie and get something to eat, okay?"

I walked into the kitchen as Nora asked, "Are you sure?"

"You don't have to do that," I offered, trying to be polite.

Darlene waved me away. "Yes, I do. You girls have been cooped up here long enough. Now get out and enjoy yourselves. It's my treat."

"Thanks!" Nora and I looked at each other and smiled. "Oh." I turned to Darlene. "But Cassidy isn't coming. She's reading *Twilight* for the first time."

Darlene chuckled. "That's a good book. I love that one. And so addictive."

My jaw dropped. "You've read *Twilight*?" *Wow. She's cooler than I thought.*

"Of course I have." Darlene looked shocked that I would

even question the statement. "I've read all the Meyer books. *The Host* is my favorite—but boy, that Carlisle is dreamy."

I grinned. I couldn't help it. "You've got a thing for Carlisle? Edward's dad?" *She's so funny.*

"Of course I do. He's a doctor. I've always had a thing for doctors," Darlene said with a wink.

"Yikes! Don't tell my dad." Nora giggled. "He's a doctor."

"Don't remind me," Darlene teased. "It's a good thing he's taken."

Nora burst out laughing. "Wow. You're awesome."

Darlene chuckled. "Do you know when you'll be back?"

Nora looked over at me, but I shrugged. "Do you think eight is too late?" she asked Darlene.

"Eight? Sure. Sounds fine to me. You've got your cell phone, right, Claire?"

"Yep. It's in my pocket." I patted the back of my jeans for good measure.

"Great. Well, then, you girls get out of here and have a good time." She shuffled us out of the kitchen and into the living room. Opening the front door, she said, "Oh, and don't forget to call if you need anything, okay?"

"Thanks," I replied just before she shut the door behind us.

"Wow, Darlene is totally cool." Nora smiled, walking toward the driver's side of a gold Dodge Crossover.

"Speaking of cool, where did you get this car?" I let my hand trail lightly across the hood. "Is it yours?"

"Yeah."

"Are you kidding me? You have your own car?" I nearly choked. Our family had two cars. If I wanted to drive, I usually got stuck with my mom's minivan.

"Well, actually, it's mine and Tony's. My parents aren't *that* nice. We have to share."

"Yeah, but still." She unlocked the door, and I climbed onto a soft leather seat. "What year is this?" The vehicle looked brand new.

She shrugged. "Last year, I think. It's not new."

"It's a lot newer than anything I've got at home." I snorted.

"Really?" Nora started the car, and the engine purred to life. "So what mall do you want? Are you a high-end shopper, or do you prefer bargains?"

I laughed. "You have to ask? Bargains, of course." My seatbelt clicked into place.

Nora looked at me funny for a moment, then smiled genuinely. "I think you and I are really going to get along."

"I hope so. We're kind of stuck with each other all day."

She glanced over briefly before looking in the rearview mirror and pulling slowly away from the curb. "You don't know my family. I love the mall we're going to, but no one else will ever come with me."

"Why?"

She rolled her eyes. "They all shop high-end."

It took me a moment to process that, but when I did, a lightbulb went on. *Tony likes expensive clothes!* If I'd have thought about it, I would've known it already. Wasn't Edward always wearing designer stuff?

Once at the mall, we cruised a bit and slurped some Orange Julius smoothies until we found one of our favorite stores—Claire's. I mean, hello, it has to be good if it's got my name.

"No way. Check out this necklace," Nora gushed as she ran over to a super-cute necklace made of green glass beads.

"Wow. That's pretty. How much is it?" I picked one up from the display hook and looked at the tag. "Shut up. It's only four bucks?"

"You do love bargains!" Nora laughed. "Wahoo!"

"Okay, so you want to know what my sisters and I do when we go to Claire's?"

"What?"

"We play this game where we each see who can find the best bargains for only ten dollars."

"Cool. Let's do it."

"But we only have ten minutes."

Nora pulled her cell out of her purse and checked the time. As soon as I did the same, she hollered, "Go!"

She won, like, totally skunked me. I couldn't believe it. She put the green necklace down and went in search of *real* bargains. Talk about cute stuff, too! I would wear all of it. Necklaces, bangle bracelets, earrings, and even an uber-cute headband. My lot was pitiful compared to hers.

"Where to next?" she said with a giggle once we'd put it all back.

"Does this mall have an Old Navy?" By far, my favorite clothing store.

"You bet! And it's really close by. Follow me."

I had to jog to catch up to her. "Man, I wish we had an outlet mall back home. This place is amazing." Not to mention huge.

"See what I mean? I swear my brother would like it if he'd give it a chance." Nora stopped in front of the store and swung out her arm dramatically. "Ta-da! Everything you could ever want from Old Navy, at a fraction of the cost."

It was like a beacon of bliss had opened up, and a choir of angels welcomed me in. I couldn't even move. My smile was so big, one of the angel's trumpets could have fallen into it, and I never would've known. "Just to warn you now, I'm never going to leave—like, ever."

"Come on." Nora chuckled and grabbed my arm, tugging me into my celestial paradise. "You haven't seen anything yet.

Wait till you check out the guys that work here."

Guys? I blinked, allowing my brain to clear from the fog. "What do you mean, guys?"

She laughed, really laughed. "Most girls only come here to check out the guys. Seriously, Old Navy is known for hiring superior specimens. Just wait."

Well, then, show me the money.

I could see exactly what she meant the moment we walked into the store. There were majorly hot guys everywhere. *Now I* know *I've died and gone to heaven.*

And that's when I saw him. The epitome of the perfect guy, walking straight toward us. Tall, built, dark hair that was a little longer than my mom liked, and dark, mysterious eyes. Those eyes connected with mine for a second, and my heart jumped into my throat.

He continued to walk toward me, and I watched as one corner of his mouth moved up in a totally sexy smile of acknowledgement. *He's checkin'* me *out, too! And he likes what he sees.* And then I heard his voice. It was like warm, melted chocolate and husky hickory bark all at the same time.

He was still looking at me when he called out, "Hey, Joe. I've got the size 8's here. Gimme a sec and I'll run them over to you." Then he stopped right in front of me.

I couldn't think. I couldn't breathe.

Joe answered back, "Sure. Don't take too long, 'kay?"

"Hmm . . ." was the reply as the hot guy's eyes searched mine before he took another step forward.

Then he wrapped me in a huge hug and whispered, "Where have you been? I tried to text you all night."

SIX

♥

SKIZZLE-SKERPED

Huh? I must be dreaming. I'm going to wake up any moment, and he's going to be gone.

My dream guy pulled back and brushed a strand of hair from my forehead. In confusion, I glanced away and caught Nora's hugely baffled look. It probably mirrored my own.

"Sadie?"

My eyes flew to his. *Save me? Did he say, "Save me"?*

"Sadie, are you going to tell me what's wrong?" he asked as he brushed another strand from my face.

Oh, Sadie! Wrong. I gulped. *He obviously thinks I'm someone else.* "I—I—" I took a deep breath and tried again. "I'm Claire." *But I could be Sadie, if you want me to be.*

"Claire?" Clearly confused, he stepped back. "Your name is Claire?"

No! "Yeah." I bit my lip.

"Are you kidding me?" He smiled, and I could feel my body melting on the spot.

"No, I'm really Claire." I grinned back.

He chuckled and brought me in for another hug. He smelled awesome. "Then why have you let me call you Sadie all this time? I feel like a major nerd now. You should've said something." He pulled back and looked at me.

"I—I—" *I never want this day to end. Ever.* "I don't know y—"

He put his finger to my lips. "Hold that thought." He must've liked the way my mouth felt, because he paused and looked down at his finger before his flirtatious eyes caught mine.

Oh. My. Gosh. I could seriously die right now. Seriously. My breath caught in my throat again. I couldn't say anything. I just nodded slightly. The action of his skin rubbing against mine sent a gazillion fairy sparkles and happy tinglings all over my mouth.

"I really, really want to finish this conversation," he said, "so could you do me a favor and wait right here? I promise I'll be back in just a sec."

His finger was still on my mouth. With that faint connection between us, there was no way I could answer him. Honestly, all of my senses were in such disarray that if breathing wasn't automatic, I'm positive my body couldn't have handled that, either. I nodded again, and my eyelashes fluttered under the torrent of sensations that exploded on my lips.

My dream guy must have noticed. He smiled that sexy half smile and mercifully dropped his finger, but then he stared intently at my mouth.

I licked my lips nervously, and in response—

He kissed me.

Ahh! I stepped back. I was so floored, I dropped my purse and my smoothie. Not kidding. My Orange Julius Raspberry Crush smoothie exploded as it hit the floor, covering everything within a ten-foot radius—including me, Nora, my dream guy, and a huge display of clothes next to us. *Oh my gosh! Oh my gosh! Oh my gosh!*

The only sound for the first two seconds was a massive gasp from Joe, the coworker my dream guy had been talking to earlier.

"Jaden!" Joe hollered once he'd found his voice. "What the heck was that?"

My dream guy stepped back, wiping wet, pink foam off his uniform. He shook his head as he surveyed the damage.

"I'm sorry. I'm so sorry," I mumbled. *Seriously, could I have been a bigger dork if I tried? I know he hates me. He has to hate me.* I *hate me!*

"I'm gonna have to go with smoothie—or milkshake—but I'm thinkin' smoothie," Jaden answered, chuckling to himself.

"You think this is funny?" Joe stormed over and stared at the mess. "Jaden, I can't believe you let your friends come in with drinks, man! You know the rules." Joe gestured to me and the display behind me. "Just look at her. She's a freak who just cost this store about four hundred dollars in damage."

People were staring. My clothes were wet. I did the only sensible thing a girl could do in that situation—I ran. Totally immature, I know. But I was so humiliated, I just didn't think properly. Instead, I pushed past a smoothie-splattered Nora and bolted out of Old Navy so fast, you'd have thought I was in a track meet.

I was almost to the entrance of the mall when Jaden caught up with me. "Claire, wait!" His hand tugged my elbow. In less than a heartbeat, I was wrapped snugly up against his warm chest again. Really, the guy was good with hugs. I was panting so hard, I couldn't have spoken even if I wanted to.

"Hey." His deep voice washed over me. "It's okay. Really,

it's okay."

I lost it. Like, really lost it. He was too nice. I always start crying after embarrassing instances when the people around me are concerned and nice about it.

"Don't mind Joe. He's a jerk sometimes. Really. I would know—I've worked with him for two years." Jaden rubbed my back gently, and I relaxed against him. "Besides," he continued, "people spill their drinks in that store every day. I'm serious. Joe was just extra cranky because ours was the third mess today."

Ours? I pulled back a little and stared at his shirt. "Uh, ours?"

"Ah! She can speak." I could hear the relief in his voice, even though I didn't look up.

"You didn't spill that stupid drink, I did."

"Yes." He lowered his head to see my eyes. "But who couldn't help himself and took you by surprise and kissed you?" He brushed a stray tear off my cheek. "And just for the record, had I been carrying a drink, I would've dropped it too."

Liar. "Really?"

His dark brown eyes, completely full of mischief, twinkled into mine. I really didn't know anything about the guy—but I didn't need to. He was wonderful. "You do realize the only thing that's stopping me from kissing you now is that I'm afraid you'll run again. Believe it or not, I have a total soft spot for tears. I can't help myself. I have to kiss them away."

"Y–you have to kiss them away?"

"Yep. You're looking unbelievably tempting right now."

"I am?"

"Oh yeah."

"Oh."

"But first things first. I think introductions are in order."

"Introductions?" My head was swimming. I could barely

keep up with his train of thought.

Jaden smiled and shook his head. "Stop. You're looking more tempting the longer I'm with you." He took two steps back—I missed his warmth the second he was gone—and held his hand out to me.

"We've never met before, have we? Wait, don't answer that." He raised his other hand. "It's obvious I've got you confused with someone else. So, let's start again."

"Obvious?" *When did he figure it out?* I ignored his hand. "But . . ."

He lowered his hand into his pocket and ran the other through his hair. "Well, yeah . . . you see, Sadie, um, I've known Sadie for like, two months now. And she's never—I mean *never*—tempted me into kissing her." Jaden put his other hand in his pocket and rocked back on his heels. The sheepish grin he gave me when he looked up nearly stole my breath away. "So, well, anyway. I figured it out as soon as I touched your lips, that you, uh, weren't her. And well, all at once, I don't know what came over me—I mean, I realized how nice you were and how much shock you must be in, since I practically attacked you, and well, something clicked. I knew I shouldn't do it, but I just wanted to kiss you. And I was going to walk away—really, I was. But then . . . then you licked your lips, and I just had to taste a sample. So, there's my confession. I'm sorry. The whole spill and everything was all my fault."

My jaw had dropped about halfway through his speech, and I still couldn't raise it. I just stood staring at him like a stupid Mary Poppins codfish. *He wanted to kiss me? Me? Even though he didn't know me—and he* knew *he didn't know me? This was better than* Twilight!

"Aw, Claire, you've gotta stop looking so cute. I'm trying to be honest with you. I don't think you realize how close you are to getting kissed again."

What does a girl say to that, anyway? "Uh, okay." I finally closed my mouth.

"Okay?" He chuckled. "Are you saying I can kiss you again?"

"No!" I blurted out. "I—I mean, er—well, whatever." *I'm such a dork.* My heart was pounding so fast I couldn't concentrate.

Jaden glanced away and then cleared his throat. He held his hand out to mine, and while shaking it, announced, "Hi, I'm Jaden. I'm seventeen. I'll be a senior this year, and I live near Seattle in a suburb about twenty minutes from here. I work at Old Navy every day except Tuesdays, Saturdays, and Sundays, and apparently, I have a new fascination with kissing girls I hardly know and terrifying them into running from me. So, uh, you're cute. What's your name?"

He looked so serious, I couldn't help it. I burst into giggles. Then I did the unthinkable—I tried to flirt back. "Hi, Jaden. I'm Claire Hart. I'm sixteen. I'll be a junior this year. But I live in Farmington, New Mexico. I'm just on a summer vacation here with my sister and some friends—"

"What? You're just visiting?" He looked so upset, I rolled my eyes. "But what am I going to do when you leave?"

"Send me an e-mail?" I giggled some more. "Or text me?" I pulled out my phone and showed it to him.

"How can I text you when I don't have your number?"

"Now, *that* was the best pickup line I think I've ever heard."

"It was good, wasn't it? Pretty sly. I think I'm going to have to use it again. Well, that is, if it works."

It worked. He looked so charmingly at me, I really didn't have a choice. After I gave him my digits, I asked, "So, do I get yours?"

"Hmm . . ." He seemed to playfully consider the idea. "Maybe. For a price."

"For a price, huh?" I put my hands on my hips. "Would that price possibly be a kiss?"

"Yeah, have to say, I think I'm headin' that way for a payment." Jaden took a step closer. My heart fluttered into my throat. "You game?" he asked.

"I—I don't know." I tried to sound cool and calm about it, but I'm not sure how well I succeeded. "I'm not sure your phone number is worth a kiss."

"What?"

"Nope." I smiled. "I'll have to see what you do with my number first, before I even *think* about kissing you again."

He took another step closer.

I stood my ground.

"Oh, I get it." He raised an eyebrow. "You're into challenges."

I thought about the bet with Cassidy and shrugged. "Sure. You could say that." I nervously licked my lips and wished I hadn't. Jaden's eyes flew to my mouth.

"What if I wanted to steal one anyway? What would you do?" he whispered as he lowered his head.

"Probably deck you," I whispered back. My chin rose a bit and my eyes fluttered closed, belying my words completely.

"I think I'll take my chances."

"Claire! Oh my gosh! There you are!" Nora hollered from somewhere behind me. I didn't care. I didn't open my eyes.

But the moment must've been ruined for Jaden, because he chuckled and murmured, "Don't worry. You'll get your kiss, I promise. And this time I'm going to deserve it."

My eyes flew open as he stepped back. I realized what a total dork I must've looked like, practically begging him to kiss me. *Sheesh.* I was so thankful for Nora.

"Are you okay?" Her eyes were huge.

"Uh, yeah. I think so," I said, wondering how much she'd seen. I refused to look at Jaden.

"You left your purse back there."

"Thank you! I forgot all about it. I'm such a moron, seriously." I looked down and saw her jeans. They were splattered with dark smoothie spots. I felt even worse.

"It's okay. Joe's not mad anymore, either. I totally told him off."

"You did?" Jaden's voice right above my head made me jump.

"Yeah." She laughed. "It was no big deal, really. I just pointedly reminded him that if he wanted to keep his job as a store manager, he shouldn't call customers names, or yell when they cause an accident. In fact, I suggested that if he continued to show disrespect and immaturity, Old Navy wouldn't even hesitate to dismiss him."

"No way!" I gaped at her, and Jaden laughed.

"Yep. He was very apologetic, too, and then admitted that all the clothes that had been 'ruined' were tax write-offs anyway."

I groaned. "Four hundred dollars' worth of tax write-offs!"

"There weren't even that many. Honest. Joe way overexaggerated, so don't feel bad. Once we cleaned up the mess, there were only a couple of shirts and a pair of jeans."

"Really?"

"I promise. Even Joe admitted that he totally overreacted. Anyway, I stayed until it was all cleared up. It only took like, max, three minutes. I just wish your purse could've made it out a little better. I think it got covered the most."

I took the soggy purse she handed me. Nora was so nice. It was obvious she'd tried to wipe off as much smoothie as she could. "Thanks. I so owe you. You've been really awesome about the whole thing." I looked down at myself for the first time and saw what a disaster I was. Even Jaden still had dark smudges all over him. He was one sticky mess. We all were. "Well, so much for the movie." I sighed. "Sorry again."

"Oh! That reminds me," Nora said. "Apparently, my speech hit home a little too hard with Joe. Maybe this isn't the first time this has happened—"

"No, it's not," Jaden confirmed.

"Well, Joe's treating us all to a new set of clothes—from his paycheck. He's hoping he'll be able to keep his job if we're nice. So what do ya say? Are you feeling nice?"

SEVEN

HIS SISTER'S KEEPER

I was feeling really nice, especially after I was wearing my new uber-cute jeans and flowing floral wrap top. Nora looked positively hot in her new jeans and ultra-light chiffon pin-tucked shirt. Even Joe noticed. Actually, for the hour or so we were in Old Navy, I saw Joe looking at Nora a lot. I mean, more than I think she realized.

"Way to go, Claire!" Nora exclaimed as we made our way out of the mall to the parking lot. "New outfits *and* a kiss. Who knew our day at the mall would get that exciting? That was just wild."

Tell me about it. "I know." I giggled in disbelief as we approached her car.

"So, I want all the gory details." She clicked her remote to unlock the car. "I mean, what were you thinking when Jaden walked up and hugged you like that?"

I opened the door and climbed in the car. "That I'd died and gone to heaven. Honestly, I didn't know what to do. Guys never, *ever* looked at me in Farmington. Not the way he was looking at me."

"And kissing you," she added. Not that she needed to—I was already thinking it.

"Seriously, could I have made a bigger fool of myself? The guy kisses me, and I freak out."

Nora began to giggle. "Okay, I know it's not funny, but boy, was it funny! Your face when he kissed you, and then his when you dumped smoothie all over him—priceless. Honestly. I so wish I'd thought to pull out my cell phone and record it."

"Gee, thanks." I fastened my seatbelt. "It's nice to know who your true friends are."

"Hey, it's not like I'd post it on YouTube" —she laughed— "that is, not right away. So, come on, you have to tell me. I mean, first off, I would've dropped my smoothie too. You have no idea. I don't know how you managed to stay standing, actually. He is hot! So, what was his kiss like? And was it just me, or was he going to kiss you again? Because when I walked up, it totally looked like he was ready to kiss you again. And when did he figure out he didn't know you?"

"Wait! You are just as bad as Chloe, my older sister. But before I answer your third-degree assault, I want to know one thing."

"Okay, what?"

"Please tell me you noticed Joe checking you out. Please just tell me you did, because that guy was doing anything and everything he could to get you to notice him."

"What? Are you kidding me? Joe?"

"Shut up! You didn't see him?"

"No," Nora said. "You're high, aren't you? Joe hates me. I mean, seriously, I threatened to get him fired. He *should* hate me. If he doesn't, then he's stupid, and I don't like stupid guys anyway."

"Whatever. He's hot, and you know it."

"Yeah, but hot *and* brainless? What's the point in that?"

"So, you're saying if he were to ask you out, you'd tell him no?" I couldn't believe it. "Even after how nice he was?"

She wiggled her eyebrows and put the car in gear. "I don't know. It'd depend on where he wanted to take me."

"You are so bad." I giggled.

"Well, I mean, who am I to pass up a free date? Come on. If he's willing to pay to get to know me a little more, I might as well oblige him."

"Admit it. You like him." I turned sideways in my seat so I could see her better as she pulled out of the parking lot.

"No way."

"Okay then, admit that you *don't* like him. Admit that you aren't the teensiest bit interested in him."

"I'm not going to admit anything."

"I knew it!" I laughed as I fell back against the seat. "You do like him. As soon as Jaden texts me, I'm going to let him know, too. I'll have you set up with Joe before you can blink."

"You wouldn't dare!" Nora's jaw dropped open.

"Chicken?"

"Claire, serious. You really think he likes me?"

"Yeah, it seemed that way. He was sure watching you the whole time you were in the store."

She changed the subject. "Okay, so it's only four o'clock. What do you want to do?"

"What do you mean?"

"You know, do some more shopping? Go out to eat? Head over to the movie now, that sort of thing?"

"Oh! Um, I don't know. Maybe we could swing by the theater and see what's playing and then go from there."

"Ooh! I got a better idea. We've got a twenty-minute drive. Why don't you call Tony and ask him what movies are playing."

"Tony?"

"Yeah, he's home right now. He can look it up for us." She handed me her phone. "Just look up call history. He should be the first or second call on there."

"Okay." It took me a minute, but I was able to find Tony Russo. I pushed the button, and he picked it up on the third ring.

"Hey, Nor. How's it goin'? Are you still with Claire? Has she mentioned me at all?"

Huh? Oh my gosh. Now what do I do?

Nora studied my shocked face. "Claire? What's wrong? Did he pick up?"

I nodded and then handed the phone over to her.

"What did you do to Claire?" she accused into the phone. "She can't even talk right now."

Yikes. I covered my face with my hands and willed myself not to think of Tony actually thinking about me and interested enough to ask if I mentioned him. I didn't succeed. *Maybe Cassidy was right. Maybe he* does *like me.*

I heard Nora laugh and looked over to see her rolling her eyes. She whispered, "He's so embarrassed right now. The dork."

I grinned. The thought of him embarrassed because of me seemed cute somehow. *Man, I'm evil.*

"Do you think you can handle talking to Claire now?" Nora teased. "What was that? You do? M'kay, let me see if she wants to talk to you." She beamed over at me. I nodded. "Here she is. Now be nice." She handed over the phone.

"Hello?"

"Sorry about that." Tony sounded sheepish.

Okay, so how cute is he?

"So, what did you need? I promise this time I won't ask you anything awkward."

"Actually, we were wondering if you could help us with something."

"Sure, no problem. What's up?"

"Well, we wanted to go to the movie later, and—"

"And you needed a really hot guy to take you?"

I smiled into the phone. "Well, there is that. Hmm . . . I'll have to think about it."

He laughed. I loved the way his laugh sounded. "What? That wasn't it? Okay, you better give me a heads-up before I make a fool out of myself for a third time today."

"We just wanted to know what movies were playing and what time." I giggled. "And since you're home and all—"

"Oh, I get it. I'm just your information service."

"Yeah, something like that."

"Fine. But it'll come with a charge."

What is it with me and guys today? "Let me guess. You want a kiss too?"

"Uh . . ." Tony chuckled into the phone. "I was thinking more along the lines of letting me go with you so I don't die of boredom here in the house all day. But hey, if a kiss is part of the deal too, who am I to complain?"

Good grief. I could feel my face go bright red. *Why did I even wake up today? I really don't think I was meant to go anywhere or speak to anyone.* I bet if I had read my horoscope that morning, it would've said something like: *A friend may plan an outing with you today. Decline. It is not in your best interest, or theirs. Also, try to keep from mingling with the opposite gender in any way. If you do, you may live to regret it.*

Also, avoid all purchased beverages. If you must, buy water.

"Claire?" Tony's deep voice reminded me that I was still on the phone with him. "You got kind of quiet after I mentioned the kiss. You're not planning to murder me now, are you?"

He surprised a giggle right out of me. "Why would I be planning a murder?" *Like I could murder a vampire if I wanted to, anyway.*

Tony laughed at my response. "Well, it's just more or less a habit with me, you know? Call me suspicious, but whenever anyone gets real quiet, I have to wonder if they're planning my demise."

I cracked up. "Your demise? What a word."

"Hey, you'd be surprised how many evil-tormenter-doomsday types live in the world today. And frankly, I don't know you from Adam. And even though I can't think of anything, I'm sure you could find a reason to get back at me. That is, if you wanted to."

"So, are you trying to tell me you're some sort of superhero, and I'm your nemesis?"

"Nemesis, huh? I like that word. It sends out all sorts of danger signals."

Danger signals? All at once, I pictured Tony kissing me, and I wondered briefly if his lips would be like Edward's—cool marble. And then, the silliest thing happened. I said something so completely baffling and unlike me. Maybe it was the recent conquest of Jaden, or the realization that Tony was interested. But whatever it was, I found myself going all movie star and using the most flirtatious line built into my subconscious that related to danger signals. "So, do you like playing with fire?"

Tony groaned temptingly. He fell for it. Hook, line, and sinker.

Fire and ice. What a concept.

After he had promised to get back to us with movie info, I hung up and went to hand the cell phone back to Nora, but she refused to take it. Actually, she looked downright peeved.

"Is something wrong?" I asked, trying to replay the last ten minutes to see if I'd said anything about her. *Did I offend her somehow?*

"You could say that." She stared straight ahead, her eyes never leaving the highway.

Great. Now what have I done? "Want to tell me about it?"

"Yep," she responded, tight-lipped. "Give me a moment, and I'll let you have it. I'm just trying to calm down first."

Calm down? I thought briefly of the facetious horoscope and growled. I *would* pick today of all days to venture out into the world.

Nora must've heard the growl, because her head whipped around and she studied me for a second before snapping her eyes back to the road. "So, what's the deal with you anyway, huh?"

"Deal?"

"Yeah. Are you just trying to get as many guys as you can while you're here, or what?"

What in the—?

"Because, you know what, if that's your game, then lay off my brother, all right? Find some other guy to bury. Because he doesn't need this, okay?"

Holy cow. Is she serious? "Nora, wait—"

"No, Claire, *you* wait! Tony is one of the best guys you'll ever meet. The most protective, nicest, caring guy ever. And if you're just trying to get him to fall for you, then congratulations, you've done it. I don't know how, when heaven knows loads of other girls have tried—but you have. So there. Game over. Now you can walk away."

“I’ve never really—”

“Don’t give me that junk, okay?” Nora was really ticked. “I heard you on the phone. As a matter of fact, I heard you on the phone just minutes after you let Jaden kiss you—almost twice!”

“Hey! I didn’t—”

“You weren’t stopping him the second time, were you?”

No.

“Look, Claire, I know we just met. And I’m sorry if I read you all wrong, especially since I don’t know what you guys are like down in New Mexico. But here, we play it pretty straight. So, whether you’re intentionally trying to go around breaking hearts or not is beside the point. The point is, you *are* breaking them, and you’re messing with my family. I don’t really like people messing with my family. So, if you like Tony, I suggest you figure it out quick and then stick with it. But don’t be playing two fields at once—not with people I care about, at any rate.”

“Whoa. You’re serious.” *Now I know how Joe must’ve felt when she yelled at him.* I decided to grovel. “Nora, honestly, I don’t even know what’s come over me today. Please believe me when I say guys have never noticed me before, and I have no idea what to do with this kind of attention, at all. What I do know for sure is that I like your brother. He has definitely intrigued me. I also haven’t seen or heard from him since Saturday. So, when today comes around, and I’m completely free and unattached, and this totally cute guy attacks me—I mean, you were there, what would you have done? And he . . . well, he can kiss. Really nicely. And he said the most amazing things to me and, well, I don’t know what’s wrong with me. I’m just way over my head.” I slumped into my seat.

Nora didn’t say anything. She didn’t even look at me.

Ugh. “Look, when I talked to Tony just now, and he flirted with me, I did something I never do—I don't even know *how* to do—I flirted back. He was so cute about it, too. He totally had my heart racing and everything. Just hearing you say that he likes me makes me totally freak out inside. But do I know which guy I like more? Sheesh. I have no idea. I'm not trying to break any hearts, that's for sure. But I really don't know either of them well enough to decide. Besides, why do I have to? I'm sixteen. It's not like I'm engaged to them. At most, they'd only be boyfriend potential for the summer, anyway."

The phone rang. It was Tony, and we both knew it. Nora looked at the cell phone sitting on the console between us and then up at me. I faced the side window.

Let her talk to her own brother. Heaven forbid, I get accused of flirting with him. If I'm lucky, he'll say the movie theater burned down so I can just go home.

EIGHT
♥
PARANORMAL ACTIVITY

"I'm sorry."

I looked over at Nora. She'd just hung up the phone with Tony.

"I'm sorry. I totally overreacted. It's just—I get a little defensive of my brother. Maybe it's because we're twins. I don't know." She sighed and set the phone between us again. "Maybe it's because every friend I've ever had has only been my friend so she could get to know him better."

"Really?"

She rolled her eyes. "Yeah. Apparently he's got some sort of fan—uh, mysteriousness—that draws females to him." She shrugged. "I don't see it, but that's what they all tell me."

I'm not the only one? "So, wait—are you saying he has tons of girlfriends?"

"No! Not at all. That's probably why I freaked out, actually. I'm saying I've never seen him really notice a girl until you."

"What?"

"Don't get me wrong. He's gone on dates and did the whole prom thing—mainly because my mom would kill him if he didn't—but other than that, he really doesn't attach himself. He says he's too busy with his career—er, I mean, school stuff—to really think about getting involved."

"No way."

"Yep. It drives girls crazy, too. I guess you could say he's sort of a challenge."

"I don't get it. If he's like that, what makes you think he's falling for me, anyway? I mean, seriously, why would he? It makes no sense."

She laughed. "Probably because you're the first girl who didn't fall all over him when you guys met. We all noticed that straight away. Even Mom and Dad teased him about it when you weren't around. It was kind of refreshing, actually, to have you want to sit next to me during the tour and not hang on him."

"But what makes you think he likes me? Sorry, but he hasn't really sent off the best signals. Besides, I wouldn't have even thought it was true until he asked about me on the phone."

"Oh, you want to know how I know he likes you." She laughed. "I forget you don't hang out at our house, so of course you wouldn't know what we all talk about—especially since you can't read minds, can you?"

Can't read minds? "Uh, no, I can't."

She giggled again. "Duh! What was I thinking? Of course you can't." She glanced over at me, her smile a direct contrast to just moments before. "We all can at home."

"You can do what?" *Sheesh. People in Seattle change subjects faster than a racecar needs its tires changed.*

"Read minds, of course."

"Are you serious?"

She laughed as if it were no big deal. "Well, that's what

Mom says, anyway. We've been doing it for years."

"Reading people's minds?"

"Finishing each other's sentences. Tony's the best at it. He can always tell what I'm thinking before I say it."

I knew it! My hand gripped the armrest of the car so tightly, my knuckles had gone white, but I didn't care. "So, I overheard you inviting Tony to come to the theater with us—is he coming?"

"Yeah." She looked awkwardly at me. "You don't mind, right? I mean, I didn't blow it between the two of you because of my outburst?"

"Blow what?" I chuckled nervously and excitedly all at the same time. "There's nothing to blow, so you're fine. I just wish Joe was coming too."

"Ah. You would. Whatever. I don't even like the guy." She chucked the phone right at me.

I caught it easily. "So, who's breaking hearts now, hmm?"

The movie was great. We decided on an animated film, since we couldn't agree on anything else. Okay, so we pushed up the average age of the audience by a few years, but it was fun. And it was really fun seeing Tony and Nora interact. They laughed just as loud—if not louder—than the little kids around us. I didn't know many teenagers who'd let loose like that. Everyone I knew was too cool to admit they still liked certain things, like cartoons.

"So, where to next, girls?" Tony's smile was really sweet as we walked out of the theater. "This is on me."

I glanced at my watch. "I don't have much time left, just forty-five minutes. Is that okay?"

"Only forty-five minutes?" He grinned wickedly and looked over at Nora. "Are you thinking what I'm thinking?"

"Yes." She giggled. "Let's do it."

"What?" I asked. *Oh my gosh, they're reading each other's minds!*

"Do you think she'd like it, though?" Tony talked over me. "Plus, do you think she's trustworthy enough?"

"Definitely. Come on, Tony, you can't get an idea like that and not do it," Nora said. "You have to now."

"Do what? What are you guys talking about?"

"You think?" He was milking it for all it was worth. "I don't know . . . she isn't technically family, you know. And usually only family gets invited."

"She's close enough. Besides, Darlene and Roger are like family."

"Close enough for what?"

"That's true." Tony looked at me. I stood between them with my hands on my hips. "Let's do it." He laughed.

"Come on," Nora tugged on my arm. "You're going to love this!"

I planted my feet right where they were. "Wait. What am I going to love? What are you guys talking about?"

Tony's smile lit up. "We're going to the park, of course."

"The—the park?" I was *so* thinking it would be something more exciting than a park.

"Yeah." He wrapped his arm around my shoulders. "It's where I used to play Little League."

"It's so much fun. Come on—say you'll come, Claire." Nora was practically jumping up and down.

The feel of Tony's strong arm on my shoulders made my head spin. I could hardly concentrate on what was happening. "A park? I have to be trustworthy to go to a park? A park where you used to play base—" I gasped. *Holy cow. A baseball park! Just like the Cullens in* Twilight. *They're taking me to play vampire baseball!* I quickly turned within Tony's arm to look up at him.

"Are—are you . . . are you sure?" I couldn't believe he was willing to take me there.

For a moment, his eyes sparkled down into mine, and I realized he wasn't saying anything. *He must be trying to read my mind!* I couldn't help it—I blushed. *Oh my gosh! Can he tell how hot I think he is right now? Seriously, up close like this, he is way cuter than Jaden. At least, I think so.* I was having a really hard time remembering what Jaden looked like at the moment.

"Hey, uh, I'm going to go get the car," Nora announced. Neither of us answered her.

"I wish I knew what you were thinking right now," Tony spoke softly as his eyes scanned my face.

I gulped. "You mean you can't tell?" I thought for sure he could.

"I thought I knew, but it can't be—it's just too good to be true. You have to be thinking something else."

"I do?"

"Claire, what *are* you thinking right now?"

That you're the most wonderful vampire in the whole world, and I would follow you to the ends of the earth if you asked me. "That I'd like to go to the park."

"Nothing else?" he teased.

"Uh—if there *is* something else, I'm going to bank on you using your intuition to figure it out."

He squeezed my shoulder and brought me in for a hug. My cheek rested against his rock-hard frame. "Deal," he muttered above my head. "But I do have to warn you, my intuition rarely fails."

"I didn't know it *could* fail." I inhaled a soft, musky scent. *Washington guys are really into hugs.*

Tony chuckled, and his whole body vibrated. "So, can I have your permission to act on whatever it is you're thinking, then?"

I pulled back so I could see him better. "What do you mean?"

"I mean, if I can tell you want to be kissed, can I kiss you?"

Washington guys think a lot about kissing, too.

Tony chuckled again. "Don't look so surprised. I'm a guy. It's all we think about. Especially when we're around a pretty girl."

Yeah, right. I rolled my eyes and pushed away from him. "So where's this place, anyway?" *Where is Nora?* I took a couple of steps forward and searched the parking lot.

"You're not going to answer my question, are you?"

I shrugged and tried to act nonchalant. "If you need to have a girl's permission to kiss her, it's not spontaneous." My knees started to shake, and I stood straighter. "And take my word for it—we all love spontaneity. It's much more exciting." I thought about Jaden and smiled.

"So, uh, you've had a lot of spur-of-the-moment kisses, then?"

I looked back and caught him kicking a small stone with the toe of his shoe. "Nope. Just one."

Tony cleared his throat and glanced up at me. "So, is that guy your boyfriend or something?"

I laughed. "Who, Jaden? No. I don't even know him. I only met him today."

Tony's eyes flashed as he raised his head. "Are you saying some guy you don't even know kissed you today?"

"Yeah. Oh my gosh, I almost had a heart attack, I was sooo freak—"

"Where?" he blurted.

"At the mall."

"At the mall? Some guy kissed you at the mall?"

"Yeah, in Old Navy."

Tony muttered something under his breath. "Where in the—where was Nora?"

"Oh, she was standing right next to me."

He lost it. "Nora was standing right next to you when some random guy walked up and kissed you?"

"Yeah. But it's okay, because he thought he knew me. Well, he didn't when he kissed me—I mean, he knew I wasn't Sadie—but when he first came up to me and gave me a hug, he thought I was this girl, Sadie."

"Wait! So this Jaden dude who was at Old Navy just walked up to you," Tony said as he walked up to me. "Just like this, and hugged you?"

"Yep. Just like that—except he was smiling."

"So, when did he kiss you?"

"Oh, when he put his finger over my mouth. He said he knew I wasn't Sadie then, because he'd never felt like kissing her when he was around her, and as soon as he touched my lips, he felt like kissing me."

"He said all this" —Tony looked down at my mouth—"while he touched your lips?"

"Oh! No. He told me that after he followed me out of the store to apologize." I decided not to mention the smoothie fiasco.

"So what happened next? After he touched your—" Tony brought his finger up and very gently caressed my bottom lip.

I froze.

His brief touch was so light, it felt like little butterfly wings before he removed his finger and ran his hand through his hair instead.

"He—he stopped and then stared at my mouth."

Tony's eyes flew back to my mouth again, and he took another step forward.

"And he made me nervous, so I licked my lips."

"You licked your lips?"

"Yeah." My actions mirrored my words as I unconsciously licked my lips again.

"And that's what made that guy kiss you?" Tony nearly whispered, his eyes never leaving my mouth.

"Yeah."

He leaned in, his mouth hovering a fraction of an inch above mine. I gasped. *Is this really happening?*

NINE

♥

BETTER THAN VAMPIRE BASEBALL

A car honked nearby, and we jumped apart. It was Nora. I heard Tony mutter something under his breath as she rolled down the electric window.

"Are you two coming or what? Hurry up. We don't have that much time."

"Okay," Tony answered as I bolted for the passenger door. *Talk about awkward.* For some reason, I was having a hard time even thinking about looking at him.

I can't believe he almost kissed me! Seriously, what is with me? Do I have some new kind of perfume on? Just the thought of almost getting kissed for the third time that day nearly drove me crazy. And to think that earlier that week, I was complaining I had never been kissed at all! *Mom would so freak out if she knew. What is it about moms and not letting their sixteen-year-old daughters kiss, anyway? Why do they all of a sudden flip out over something so small—and okay, not meaningless, since we all know kisses mean a whole bunch? But honestly, what is the big deal?*

"So, are you ever going to forgive me for honking?" Nora giggled in the seat next to mine.

I heard Tony move behind us. "I don't know. Maybe."

His sister burst into laughter. "You know you deserved it! What were you thinking, anyway?" she asked the rearview mirror.

I looked out the window and tried to ignore her.

"Just drop it, and get us to the park, okay?" he said.

"Drop it?" She laughed again as she pulled away from the curb. "Ha. This is way too good. Especially after all the times you've teased *me* about kissing. Oh, heck no. This is going down in the Hall of Records."

Tony groaned. "You're kidding, right? I was only playing with you, Nora. Come on. Don't do this."

"Just like I'm only playing with you now?" she retorted, then turned to me. "So, you'll never guess what my brother has given me a hard time about since I kissed my very first boyfriend."

I rubbed my hand over my eyes and shook my head. *Just leave me out of this.* When I looked up again, she was waiting. "Gee, could it be kissing?" I said.

"Yep!" She laughed at Tony's groan. "But not just that. I wouldn't be giving him such a hard time now, if it was just that. Nope—"

"Nora!" he growled from behind. "I will get you back—"

"It'll be worth it." She smirked into the mirror, then glanced my way again. "Tony's got virgin lips."

"Virgin lips? Tony?" I didn't dare glance back at him.

"Yep. My brother, the playboy—the guy every girl dreams of kissing—has never kissed a girl. Can you believe it?"

No way.

"You are so going down," he mumbled.

"And surprisingly, until recently—very recently—he has been opposed to the idea altogether. In fact, he's actually had the audacity to rebuke me for kissing my boyfriends."

"Ah, man! That's because you couldn't care less about them!" he nearly shouted behind me. "Besides, you know what I said, anyway. I said I'd never kiss a girl I didn't feel—uh . . ." He stopped.

"Feel what, Tony? What were you going to say? I'm sure Claire would love to know."

Oh my gosh.

"Feel like I—uh, knew that well," he finished lamely.

Nora snickered. "Don't buy it, Claire. He's always said he'd never kiss a girl he didn't feel he could love." Then she added, "Which is why I had to stop you. There's no way you know Claire enough to decide you could love her. Trust me. You'll thank me for this someday." He mumbled under his breath again as Nora sighed. "Don't worry about us. Tony and I argue all the time," she explained to me. "I just rarely have the upper hand. So in case you think I'm being extra mean, just ask him—he'll tell you he totally deserves it. Don't you, Tony?"

He grunted. "Hmm . . . probably."

Nora was all smiles as she pulled into a parking lot and cried out in a taunting, sing-song voice, "Oh, look! We're here."

I breathed a sigh of relief, and I think Tony did too.

It was awkward when he helped me get out of the car, but he was pretty big about it. I mean, he seemed less embarrassed than I did.

He grinned ruefully. "Hey, sorry about Nora. You okay?"

"Me? Yeah, I'm fine. Are you?"

"Wow. That's refreshing." His light brown eyes sparkled into mine.

"What is?" I couldn't help but smile.

"Are you always this nice?"

"Nice? I don't know. Isn't everyone?"

"Ha!" He shut the car door behind me. "You *are* nice if you think that."

"I am?" For some reason, the thought of Tony thinking I was nice wasn't weird at all.

"Yeah." He glanced down at me, then out toward the park. "And to answer your question, yes, I'm fine. I'm actually kind of relieved. Nora could've done a lot worse, had she wanted to."

"She could?" I couldn't imagine anything more embarrassing than what he'd just gone through.

His eyes caught mine again. "Oh yeah. She's got a lot more ammunition to use. I've given her a ton of grief over the years." He sighed. "I guess its payback time. But something tells me you'll be worth it."

"Oh." My heart melted. In fact, my whole insides resembled something just short of jelly.

"Will you two knock it off and get over here?" Nora hollered from behind me.

"That'd be our cue." I smiled.

"Is it? Do we have to go?"

How cute is he? "I'm thinking so. If not, she may start whippin' out the big guns."

"Big guns?" He chuckled. "Is that something they say down in New Mexico?" He held out his hand and took mine. I didn't resist.

His hand was a bit colder than mine, but warmer than marble. "My ancestors were gunslingers."

"Really? Like outlaws?"

"Some of them." His hand was warming up really fast. I brought it up to see it properly.

"What's wrong?"

"Your hand." I turned it over. I never noticed before, but with my fingers interlaced with his, I could see he was about as tan as I was.

"What about it?"

"It's warm."

"Yeah? It usually is in the summer."

"And it's darker than I expected."

"Really? You had expectations about my hand?"

What?

"Does this mean you've been thinking about holding it?"

Ugh! How do I get myself in these situations? "Um . . ." I felt my face go as red as a tomato.

Tony laughed and tugged me forward. "Now, come on, before Nora throws something at us."

So I was surprised again—completely surprised—when we passed the baseball diamond and headed toward the playground equipment.

"We're going to the swings?" I asked.

"Nope." Tony chuckled. "You'll see."

I raised my eyebrows as we passed the playground equipment altogether. *Where are we going?* We stopped in front of a huge drinking fountain that looked like a bear. I was a bit concerned. "We came here to get a drink?"

"No, silly." Nora laughed. "We came here to play on *that!*"

I looked over to where she was pointing. Beyond the drinking fountain and to the left a bit was a ginormous zip line. "Wow! Are you kidding me?"

"Do you guys have these in New Mexico?"

"I think they were banned like twenty years ago. I've always wanted to try one, though!" I had already begun walking toward it, Tony easily keeping pace.

"Well, this is your lucky day!" Nora exclaimed as she jogged to catch up to us.

"How do they work?" The zip line seemed longer the closer I came to it.

"It's easy," Tony said. "You'll catch the hang of it right away."

"Yeah, and I bet Tony won't mind helping you at all," Nora teased.

There was a little girl climbing onto the zip line with the help of her father as we approached. I watched her sit on the circular seat and wrap her legs around the chain that attached it to the line. Her dad pulled her slowly to the top of the little hill and then counted to three. With a *swoosh* and a squeal, she zipped past us in a flash and then slowed once the line made it to the other side and started climbing that hill. In no time at all, the swing had lost its momentum, and the girl started to glide back toward the center of the line. Her father met her there, and when she begged him to let her go again, he announced, "No, you've had your turn. These people want to play, too." He pointed at us, and the little girl glanced over. "See? It's their turn now. Besides, it's time for us to head home."

I could see she wanted to argue more, but with an audience, she kept quiet.

"Thanks." I smiled and waved, hoping she would feel better.

I think it worked. She smiled and waved back as they walked past us. "Hold on real tight, 'kay?" she said to me.

"I will," I promised with a chuckle. I glanced at my friends. Both of them were staring at me. "What?"

"You like kids, too, don't you?" Nora asked.

"Uh, sure. Doesn't everybody?"

Tony smiled a huge smile, and Nora groaned. "Would you have one flaw, please? Please?" she said. "You're making me feel like an ogre."

"An ogre? Why?"

"Don't mind her." Tony gave my hand a squeeze. "Kids drive Nora crazy."

"Oh. Do they bug you, too?" I asked him.

Nora huffed. "Tony? Mr. Youth Club Volunteer Extraordinaire? I wish. That's why you haven't seen him this last week, by the way. He's been out volunteering the past few days. He would've been gone today, but they didn't need him."

He shook his head. "Come on, stop boring her. Let's get moving or Claire won't have time to try it out." He turned to me. "Do you want to go first?"

"Me?" I squeaked. "Uh, why don't I watch you guys, and then I'll try it."

"Wahoo! I'm first!" Nora shouted as she ran to the swing.

She was a natural. I could tell she'd been playing on the zip line for years. She and Tony made it look easy. By the time it was my turn, I was positive it was the simplest thing I'd ever do.

That was until I tried to balance myself on the little disk they called a seat. I actually fell off three times just getting on—to the delight and laughter of the Russo twins—before I was able to gain my balance enough to head up the hill.

Nora and Tony pushed me up to the top, and we were all laughing.

"How did you guys make this look so easy?" I gasped as I felt the jolt of the glider hit the top of the zip line.

"It's because it *is* easy." Tony chuckled. "It's just that you Southwesterners have to do everything the hard way."

"Hey. I'm not as tall as you guys," I protested. "There was no way I could get on up here, and you know it. My only chance was getting on below and having you guys push me up."

"Excuses, excuses," Nora said with a grin. "Now, are you ready?"

No. I squealed and hung on to the chain with all my might, my eyes closed and everything. "Okay."

"One," Tony said near my ear. "Two, threeee—"

They let go, and I flew down to the bottom of the zip line and back up the other side—screeching like a banshee the whole way. The metal clinked against the top, and I jolted to a stop and then was slowly dragged down to the middle again.

Nora and Tony raced down the hill to meet me. "How was it?" he asked. "You want to go again?"

"Are you kidding me?" I gasped as I opened my eyes for the first time. "That was awesome! I never want to get off!"

Honestly, this is way better than watching someone else play baseball, even if they are vampires and can run at the speed of light. It's much more fun to swing at the speed of light than to watch someone else do it, right?

TEN

OVERRULED

"You know, you might actually get your text messages if you took *your* phone with you and not mine," Cassidy announced as I walked through the front door. She was sitting on the couch in the little living room, waiting for me.

"What?" I took my purse off my shoulder and tossed it onto the end table next to her, then pulled my phone out of my back pocket. "I've got it right here."

"Really? Open it up."

I did. Cassidy's background picture flashed on the screen. *Oh, no.* I looked up. She was holding my phone out in front of her, dangling it between two fingers.

"Of course, I'm awfully curious to find out who this 'J' is who's been texting you all night."

"Shut up! Are you serious? Jaden's been texting me?" I threw her phone at her and dove for mine. She was quicker than me, keeping it just beyond my reach. "Hey! Give me that."

"You know, he's been the most interesting thing to happen

to me all day. Well, that and finally finishing your book."

"Cass, hand me the phone. You're not funny."

"I will, once you tell me about this kiss he's been going on about."

"You've been reading the texts?"

She giggled and scrambled to her feet as I lunged toward her again. "And writing back to him."

"What?" *Ugh.* "That is seriously not cool. What have you been saying to him, anyway? Give me that!" With one final lunge, I yanked my phone out of her hands.

"See for yourself." She was still giggling. "He sounds pretty hot."

As quick as I could, I pulled up my messages. "Did you tell him you were my sister?"

"Nope. He thought I was you the whole time." She smirked evilly as she plopped back on the couch. "Serves you right—taking my phone so I couldn't talk to any of my friends."

In disgust, I wandered over to the matching chair and plunked down. As far as I could tell, they'd had quite a huge conversation. Jaden alone had sent at least ten texts.

I can't believe my sister is such a loser.

"You're so rude," I grumbled as I scrolled to the beginning and started reading.

> hey, wantd 2 say srry agn. miss u
> already. cant wait 2 touch ur lips
> agn.
> J

Aw. How romantic is that? I grinned and then read Cassidy's answer.

It's nice to be missed... So what
are you talking about? What do
you mean touch my lips again?
—princessC

Did he tell her? I quickly scanned his reply.

u no what. the kiss. its all ive bn
thnkn about.

Really? I bit my bottom lip to stop the smile that was spreading across my face, then quickly read the next message from Cassidy, worried she'd freaked out. Thankfully, she was cool about it.

Good grief. Boys. *rolls eyes*
—princessC

lol. so what ya doin now?

Reading. You? —princessC

really? me im playin a game w my
lil bro.

No way! He has a little brother?

Cool. How old is he? —princessC

hes 10 and kickn my butt. what
book u readin?

I chuckled as I read Cassidy's reply.

> Lol. You probably need your
> butt kicked. I'm reading Twilight.
> —princessC

> ug! twilight? my sis wood luv u. its
> all she reads. Lame

Huh? Whatever, dork! I know he did not just say that!

> Seriously. You think it's lame?
> —princessC

> come on. u have 2 admit it. don't
> say u like it 2

She better have said I liked it.

> You're treading on thin ice. I
> suggest you change the subject.
> You don't want to deal with the
> wrath of Claire. Trust me, it's not
> pretty. —princessC

> Lol. Fine. I give, you win. So what r
> u doin 2morrow? Wanna hang?

Oh my gosh! He asked me out?

> Sure. Gotta see if you deserve
> another kiss or not. —princessC

Kiss? Kiss? She would *have to say that.* I glared up at her then quickly read his reply.

> great. c u at 6 then. whats ur addy?
> ill pick u up tomorrow.

Are you kidding me? "No!" I turned to Cassidy. "I have a date with Tony tomorrow night. He's taking me to his youth club for a game he's coaching. Dang it, Cass. Why'd you tell Jaden I'd see him?"

She rolled her eyes and pushed herself off the couch. "Will you knock it off already? If you'd think about it, I totally did you a favor."

"How? You can't set me up with someone else. Seriously, that's not fair."

"Just tell Tony you can't make it and you'll go to his next game. I'm sure there are tons. Besides, J's already got the tickets. You can't back out on him."

"Got the tickets for what?" I scrolled down to the next text.

> k ur never gonna blieve this. i jst
> pict up tkts 4 mariners game! U like
> bsbll rite?

Ugh. Only when it's vampire baseball. How much did those tickets cost?

> Wow! Cool. Baseball rocks. It
> sounds like fun! —princessC

> awesome! c u later.

J

This is not happening to me. This is not happening to me! When I looked up again, my sister had left. *Man, why didn't I bring my stupid phone with me?* I really didn't want to cancel on Tony, but it looked like I had to.

In frustration, I scrolled through my phonebook for the number he'd just given me. It took two tries before I realized I had saved his number to my sister's phone. "Cassidy!" I called, bolting up the stairs. "I need your phone!"

By the time I had Tony's number safely stored on my phone and erased from Cassidy's, I noticed it was almost nine o'clock. Completely nervous, I selected his number and pressed "send."

"Hello?"

"Hi, Tony? This is Claire."

"Oh, hey, Claire. I just told my dad about you coming tomorrow."

"You did?" *Good grief. How much harder does this have to get?*

"Yeah, he thinks it's cool. What's up?"

"Oh, well, I—uh, I can't go with you tomorrow. I got home, and Cassidy had already planned stuff for me that I didn't know about. I'm really sorry."

"Oh, hey, no worries. I hear you on the family involvement issues."

"You do?"

"Yep. Mine is always planning stuff without asking first. Drives me nuts."

"I really wanted to go, though. Can we do it another day?"

"Sure. The next game is Saturday. What are you doing then? Can you make it?"

"Um, nothing that I know of. Hang on." I put my hand over

the mouthpiece, then walked down the hallway and knocked softly on the Hadleys' bedroom door.

"Yes, dear?" came the reply.

"Sorry. It's Claire. Are you guys awake?"

"Yep. Come on in."

Hesitantly, I pushed the door opened and poked my head in the room.

Roger and Darlene were both wide awake and watching a crime show on TV. Their room was even bigger than ours and had its own little cozy sitting room off to the side.

"What did you need?" Darlene asked. "Did you have a good time today with Nora?"

"Yes. And actually, I'm talking to Tony right now." I held up the phone so she could see. "He was wondering if I could go with him to the youth center on Saturday. We're not doing anything, are we?"

"Not that I know of." She turned to her husband. "Do you know of anything going on Saturday, dear?"

"I have a luncheon meeting, but that's it."

"See, perfect," Darlene said. "Tell Tony you can go with him."

"Okay, thanks! Good night."

"Night," she called out as I shut the door.

"Okay, Tony, I can go."

"Great! You're going to love it. The game's at eleven on Saturday, okay? So I'll be there around ten."

"Sounds great. I'll bring my umbrella, just in case."

"Yeah, soccer in Washington can get wet. Very wet." He chuckled. "Did you have fun today?"

"Of course! It's been one of the craziest, most fun days I've had since coming here. I had a blast."

"Oh yeah, I forgot. You got kissed today, too, didn't you?"

I decided not to answer that.

"I'm going to have to meet that guy someday."

"Oh." I couldn't quite picture Jaden and Tony in the same room together. It sort of terrified me, actually.

"What's he look like?"

"Who, Jaden?"

"Yeah."

"Um, I don't really remember."

Tony burst into laughter. "You're kidding me. You don't remember what the guy looked like? Not much of a kiss then, was it?"

All at once, Jaden's kiss came back to me full force. I remembered every bit of it. And it was a pretty darn good one, thank you very much. "He has brown hair and dark brown eyes, and he's a bit taller than you. There. That's all I remember." *And he's totally hot.* Not that Tony wasn't hot, because he was. It's just that Jaden was a different sort of hot—a more shocking, outrageous, brave sort of hot. Tony was definitely the more cautious of the two.

"Well, I guess I better let you go," he nearly choked into the phone.

Oh my gosh! I wonder if he heard my thoughts? Dang. "Okay. I'll see you later. Sorry again. I'm looking forward to Saturday."

"Good night," Tony answered right before I heard the phone click.

"See?" Cassidy smiled from her bed as I walked into the bedroom. She must've heard everything I'd said. "That wasn't so bad, now, was it?"

I sneered at her and tossed my phone on the bed. "No thanks to you."

"You'll thank me after you've gone out with Jaden tomorrow,

I promise. You're gonna let me meet him, aren't you?"

{♥}

My date with Jaden was different from anything I had ever experienced. Not that I'd been on many dates. Okay, so this was the very first. But I was certain this wasn't what a dating experience was meant to be!

"Um, are you sure we should be going seventy-five in a thirty-mile-an-hour zone?" I asked timidly as I held on for dear life. We were speeding through a neighborhood, and I knew that at any minute, we were going to hit something.

Jaden laughed. "What are you worried about? I'm the best driver in the whole world." He dodged a skittish cat, and the car swerved wildly to the right.

I freaked. "You almost killed that cat!"

"No way. The cat stopped."

"But what if it hadn't?"

"It did, so stop worrying about it." Jaden turned the radio up louder. Rap music filled his older model sports car. The pounding bass only added to my confusion. "So, what do you think of my car?" he hollered over the music, looking smug.

Apparently I was supposed to say it was the best car in the world. "Um—" Thankfully, I didn't have to answer as we swerved to avoid a trash can that'd been knocked over.

Jaden swore loud enough to be heard over the music, then called to me, "What is that? Why can't people pick up their crap, anyway?"

"Maybe you should slow down." *Please slow down.*

"No way! This car loves to fly! She goes a lot faster, too. Wanna see?"

When I yelled, "No!" he revved up the engine and laughed.

And drove faster.

I checked my seat belt for the tenth time since getting in the car. It was fastened. Nervously, I clutched my phone, ready to dial 9-1-1 at any moment.

"Besides, this is a shortcut. You'll see. We'll get there much faster this way."

"Yeah, but funny thing is, I'd rather get there alive!" I was beginning to lose my cool. What is it with guys and risking lives to show off, anyway?

Just then, a little kid rode his bike into the street right in front of us.

"Holy—!" Jaden jerked the steering wheel. The car missed the boy by mere inches, then whipped wildly back and forth.

I lost it. "Jaden! Stop the car now. I'm getting out."

"What? Why?"

I turned off the radio. "Because, you idiot. I don't want to be a part of an involuntary manslaughter case! When you go to court, it'll be your butt that ends up in the slammer, not mine." He didn't pull over, but he did slow down. I didn't care. I was mad. "Stop this car!" When he ignored me, I flipped my phone open and began to dial.

"What are you doing?" he bellowed. The car screeched to a halt. My seatbelt jerked against my shoulders, and I came within an inch of hitting the dashboard.

In two seconds flat, I was out of my seatbelt and scrambling out of the car. By the time I had slammed my door shut, he had gotten out of the car too and was standing there with his door wide open.

I glared at him over the top of the roof.

"What is your problem?" The look he gave me could've soured milk. "Who were you calling, anyway?"

I held up the phone. "The cops."

He swore a whole slew of profanity and thumped his hand down on the roof. "Are you kidding me? For what?"

"For what? For *what?* Are you for real?" I stepped forward and banged my hand down on the roof too. "For abduction and dangerous driving, that's what!"

"For abduc—are you kidding me?" He looked away and yanked his hand through his hair. "You know, I thought you were really cool. I guess I was wrong. Excuse me, but I didn't realize I had a little lawyer in my car."

"A little lawyer?" That did it. I hitched my purse up on my shoulder and started walking back the way we'd come. *There is no way I'm getting into the car with that loser again. I can't believe I actually gave up my date with Tony for this. Jaden is an egotistical moron!*

Thank goodness I had my tennis shoes on. I had a long walk ahead of me.

ELEVEN

♥

THE GREAT ESCAPE

"Claire."

Jaden's voice sounded repentant, but I didn't care. I walked faster.

"Claire, come on!"

I ignored him.

"For crying out loud, you're blowing this way out of proportion. Now come back."

Come back? As if I'm some dog he can call and I'll come running? Maybe they do that here, but girls from Farmington don't take that kind of—

"Claire!" I could hear him jogging to catch up. "Look, I'm sorry, okay?"

I kept walking.

He swore again.

You know, you catch a lot more flies with honey than you do with swear words.

He caught up. "What do you want from me?" His stride had

to shorten to keep pace with mine.

That is so annoying. Why is he so tall, anyway? "Go away, Jaden," I huffed as I picked up my pace. It was useless—he didn't even have to try hard to match it. Speed walking was so not a talent of mine. I probably looked like a dork, but I didn't care. There comes a point when you realize your life is more important than how stupid you look. I was at that point.

"Claire, seriously, I'm really sorry, okay?"

Do not give in. Do not give in.

"You're right. I acted like a total jerk back there. I'm sorry. Now will you get back in the car?"

"No."

He sighed but didn't protest. Instead, he put his hands in his pockets and strolled along while I panted next to him.

Just go away. Sheesh.

"So, where are you going, anyway?" He sounded amused, like he thought this was cute or something.

"Anywhere that's away from you."

"That'll be kind of hard," he had the audacity to point out. "Looks like I'm staying right next to you."

Ugh. I nudged him with my elbow. "Go away."

He chuckled at my attempt, but then answered seriously, "I can't."

"Yes, you can," I growled at him. "Now leave me alone."

"Claire, I don't care how mad you get, I'm not leaving you alone in this neighborhood. So forget it." He seemed really pleased with himself, like I was supposed to congratulate him for suddenly remembering to be a gentleman.

The dork!

"You know what?" I stopped and put my hands on my hips. "I don't need anyone to take care of me, okay?" I stomped my foot for good measure.

Jaden looked down at that foot and stifled a grin.

I could've cheerfully decked him. "I'm serious!" I snapped. "Go away."

"Look." He folded his arms and glanced down the road. His car was about five hundred yards away. "I'm Native American. We stick together."

"What?" I looked at him again, really hard. "You're Native American?" It was like he had just punched me in the gut. "Are you serious?" *Why haven't I noticed before?*

"Do you have a problem with that?" He seemed confused.

"What? No, no!" I shook my head. "I have a lot of Navajo and Hopi friends in Farmington. What tribe are you from?" I had to ask, even though I knew the answer before he said it—

"Quileute."

Oh my gosh. No wonder he was driving like a maniac—not caring about anyone. No wonder he's so flippin' tall. No wonder he doesn't listen to anything I say. And that totally explains why he just grabbed me and kissed me yesterday. Jaden's a werewolf! Just like Jacob Black in Twilight. *Holy cow! How did this happen to me? Me!*

"What's wrong, Claire? You look like you've seen a ghost."

"Jaden, what's your last name?"

"Black. Why? What's—?"

I didn't hear the rest.

I fell.

"What do you mean, Jaden's a werewolf? What are you talking about? There are no werewolves in the book anyway. What in the world gave you that idea?" Cassidy stopped pacing and turned toward me. "You know what I think? I think you hit your head harder than you thought."

"I didn't hit my head. Jaden caught me before I fell all the way down."

"You are such a weirdo, Claire, you know that? A weirdo." She continued pacing. "I can't believe we were even raised in the same family. Look, just do me a favor and don't tell people we're related, okay?"

"Cass, I'm serious. He's a werewolf."

"He is *not!"* She walked right up to my bed, to which Darlene had sentenced me for the rest of the day, thanks to my collapsing episode. "You get it right out of your mind this instant! Do you hear me? Stop thinking you live in a book, okay?"

"Cassidy, just because you can't see the possibilities around you, doesn't mean other people are blind. Jaden Black *is* a werewolf! He is. I'm positive of it. You should've seen him—"

"Will you knock it off?" She marched over to the dresser, pulled out *Twilight,* and threw the large black book on my bed. "I read it, okay? I can see where you might've thought Tony was a vampire. I can see that." She raised her hand when she saw my excitement. "It doesn't mean he is. I can just acknowledge where you caught the idea that he might be one. Sheesh, after reading the book, even I wish he was." She walked over to her bed and sat down, trying another tactic. "But, honey—" she smiled a brief, sad smile "—there's nothing in that book to give any evidence that Jacob Black is a werewolf. Nothing. Just because he's Native American and understands earth and nature a lot more than we do, does not make him a werewolf. Honestly, I don't know—"

"That's it!" I threw the covers off and jumped out of bed.

Cassidy gasped. "Where are you going? You can't get up. You're not allowed. Darlene said I had to make sure you stayed in bed."

"Oh, please. I'm not sick." I walked over to the closet and yanked out my luggage. "So I got a little woozy." After throwing the suitcase on the floor, I unzipped the front pouch. "There's no reason for everyone to treat me like a little baby." *A-ha!* With a sharp tug, I pulled out book two in the Twilight saga—*New Moon,* the book that introduces and describes everything werewolf related. "Here." I tossed it across the room.

She had to stretch to catch it. "What's this?"

"Book two. You've only read book one." I grunted a bit as I zipped up the suitcase and shoved it in the closet.

"Are you kidding me? You actually lugged this out here, too?" She turned it over in her hands. "How many books did you bring, anyway?"

"All four."

"You brought four huge books like this on vacation? You *are* out of your mind."

"Yep. I had to. It's the whole series." I slumped back onto my bed and ordered, "Now read."

Cassidy groaned.

"You *do* want to know what happens to Bella and Edward, don't you?"

She rolled her eyes but ran her fingers gently over the red and white flower on the cover.

"Read. And hurry up, because I need your help."

"Knock knock," Darlene called through the door.

I quickly jumped under the covers. "Come in."

She carried in a large tray with a plate of sandwiches on it. "I heard you girls up here talking, so I figured you were awake now." She smiled at me.

I wasn't asleep. I hadn't *been* asleep. And I wasn't *going* to sleep! "So, is Jaden gone?" I asked sweetly as I sat up and straighten the covers, making way for the food. Then, as an afterthought I added, "Thank you for dinner."

"No worries." Darlene clucked. "You poor thing. How are you feeling now? Better?"

Worse. She still hadn't answered my question about the lying, two-faced, double-crossing, no good . . . "Is Jaden still here?"

Darlene's smile slipped as she glanced over at Cassidy. "Well, Cass, would you like a sandwich? I made some for you, too."

"He *is* here, isn't he?" If I tried, I could probably smell him, *the . . . the dog. Ugh. If he so much as even tries to come up here, I'll—*

"Yes, dear." Darlene wouldn't meet my eyes. In fact, she hadn't met my eyes since I'd had my huge blow up downstairs, when Jaden carried me into the house. *As if I needed to be carried by such a pompous jerk. I would rather walk barefoot on broken glass than be held by that imbecile.* I still couldn't believe he had the guts to try and kiss me again, too, right as he was carrying me up the steps to the cottage, telling me I looked so cute and smelled so good that he wasn't going to be able to help himself. Thank goodness Darlene opened the door when she did—it was the only thing that saved him.

In disgust, I shook my head. *Seriously, if he ever tries that again, I'll bite his lips off!*

Darlene brushed the comforter with her hands. "I know you don't want to talk to Jaden right now." She tried to smile again. "But I don't think he's leaving until you at least say something to him. He's pretty worried about you—you gave him quite a fright, falling down in the middle of the street like that."

At least I should be grateful nobody's calling it fainting. Not that I did faint—I'm sure I didn't. Okay, so there were a few moments I couldn't remember, like actually being caught by Jaden. I didn't remember that at all. I remembered being in his arms on the sidewalk, and I remembered him freaking out, but I don't remember getting back into the car. I can vaguely recall some of the drive, but I don't think I fully came to my senses until the moron had the gall to try to kiss me again on that stupid front porch.

Darlene was still talking. ". . . it's okay, though. He's on the phone with your parents now, and I'm sure—"

"Excuse me. Who's on the phone with my parents?"

She gave me a sympathetic look. "Jaden, dear."

"Jaden? Jaden Black is on the phone with my parents right now?" *What in the world?* "Send him in, please." I smiled to reassure her, but I don't think it worked. "I want to talk to him." That did it. Obviously, Darlene was all about getting us to speak to each other.

"Okay." She fluttered around the room and tidied a couple of things. "I'll send him right up."

"Uh, I'll go see if Mom wants to talk to me," Cassidy suggested. I could tell she would rather be anywhere but in here when I let Jaden have it.

"Okay. Great." Darlene was all smiles now, and her eyes finally met mine. "He'll be so happy you want to talk to him, I'm sure. He's been so worried. And he seems like the nicest guy. If I had a daughter, I would—oh, never mind. Let me go get him for you."

"Thanks." I thought my smile would crack under the strain as she left.

How dare that little—er, big—weasel worm his way into my friends' and family's hearts! How dare he talk to my parents and reassure them. That's all I need—everyone falling for the werewolf! The reckless, wild, Anger Management Anonymous werewolf! Great. Fabulous. Just back-flippin' dandy.

I sighed as I heard his heavy footsteps creak up the stairs.

What would Bella have done in my shoes?

TWELVE
♥
VAMPIRES, WEREWOLVES, AND ME . . . OH MY!

"Hey, you." Jaden peeked his head into the room. "Is it safe now?"

Depends on your definition of "safe." "Sure, come in." *I don't eat wolf, anyway.*

"Darlene says you're feeling better." He walked in, and I gasped to see his head almost brushing the slanted ceiling in places.

"How tall are you?"

He shrugged and grinned. "I don't know. Last time we checked, I was around six three. Why?"

"Just curious." His smile was pretty cute. It was the same smile he used on me the first time I saw him. "Why aren't you watching the Mariners game? I thought you'd be long gone by now."

"Nope. I have some things I needed to sort out with you first."

Well, that makes two of us, buddy. I pointed to the stuffed chair across the room. "Have a seat." After he sat down, I asked, "So, who did you talk to, my mom or my dad?"

"Ah—that's why you've had a sudden change of heart. Both."

Both? Ugh! I smiled sweetly. "Really?"

"Yep. They're both pretty nice, too. Except your mom's a bit concerned, of course."

"Of course." *I'm sure you told her every gory detail.*

"Especially once she learned about your fascination with werewolves."

My jaw dropped. *What? He heard that? He told my mom that? Dang!* "How did you—?"

"Know?" he finished, one eyebrow raised flirtatiously as he leaned forward in the chair. "About your fascination with werewolves? Hmm . . . could it be your love of *Twilight*? Or wait, maybe it's Native Americans. Or could it possibly be my last name, Black?"

He's good. He's really good. "So, you figured it out?"

"The reason why you fainted? Yeah—"

"I did not faint!"

Jaden chuckled as he pulled himself out of the chair and stalked over to my bed, his dark eyes glittering dangerously. All of a sudden, I found myself wishing I wasn't alone. He *was* a werewolf, after all, and everyone knows their moods change extremely fast. He prowled right up to me and leaned over.

"Yes, you fainted." His eyes hungrily devoured my face, and I gulped. "You're really lucky I like you, because I could've eaten you right there on the street."

"Really?" My eyes were huge.

He gave me a slow, sexy smile and leaned down farther. I sank into my pillows. *Do something. Scream. Bite. Push. Something. Why in the world are you frozen? Only vampires are frozen!* That did it. Just as I opened my mouth to scream, Jaden covered it with his.

Oh my gosh! About ten rapid heartbeats pounded before he released me.

"Got it," he whispered above my lips. "I told you I'd kiss you again."

"Ugh!" I growled.

He smirked, still hanging above me. "And you didn't even push me away."

I was pushing now, but he was ignoring me. He lowered the scant few inches to kiss me once more, but this time I was prepared. With a glare, I bit him. Hard.

"Holy—!" The slew of foul language that escaped from Jaden's mouth as he jerked away from me would've made a sailor blush. I wasn't a sailor. My face stayed stone cold. In fact, I was ticked. I was more than ticked. This was my turn for talking. I invited him up to my room to discuss things on *my* terms.

What in the world does that idiot think he's doing, trying to kiss me in my bed?

If my daddy were here, Jaden Black would've been thrown outside on his head—werewolf or not. Boys weren't allowed anywhere near our bedrooms at home.

Now I know why. The jerk.

"Are you through?" I smiled a short, tight smile at him.

"Holy mother of Pete's sake!" He made an obvious attempt to curb his temper as he stomped around, covering his mouth with his hand. "What'd you do that for, huh?"

"That was only your bottom lip. Come near me again and I'll bite your other one," I stated calmly.

"You wanted me to kiss you! I could tell."

The nerve. I took a deep breath to stay cool. "No. I didn't. In fact, I was pushing you away."

"You're lucky you didn't draw blood." He gingerly touched the swollen lip.

"No, *you're* lucky I didn't draw blood." I took an exasperated breath. It was ridiculous, going in circles with this guy. "What did you say to my parents, anyway?"

"Nothing." He stomped over to the chair and plopped down. "I was just teasing you about the werewolf stuff."

"You mean you didn't tell my mom?"

"That you thought I was a werewolf? No." He leaned forward and pointed to his lip. "Do you see this? Do you? If I were a werewolf, my lip would already be healing!" He slumped back angrily into the chair. "No thanks to you, I've gotta walk around like this for forever now."

"Oh, please." I folded my arms. "Besides, if you're that mad at me, what are you still doing here?"

"Good point. I have no idea, really." He grunted and stretched his long legs out in front of him. "Since I've met you, my whole life has turned upside down. For some reason I must enjoy this torture—because beyond my gut instincts to run as far away as I can, I find your train-wreck possibilities fascinating. And believe it or not, somewhat endearing. I mean, what other guy can say he's had smoothie dumped on him, tears smeared all over his shirt, a shouting match in the middle of Bluebird Avenue, a fainting scare, werewolf accusations, and a bitten lip, all within a forty-eight-hour period? See what I mean? I must be attracted to danger."

Good grief. "You're not attracted to danger, just attention. And if you don't start behaving properly, I'm going to give you some more attention, and I promise you won't like it."

"You know, you're starting to sound like my mom."

"Good! I'm glad to know that at least one of us is mature around here."

He grunted and scrunched down lower in the seat, but didn't answer.

"So, when did you read *Twilight*?" I asked him. "And who

had to bribe you to do it?"

"No bribes. Just got tired of hearing my mom and sisters talking about this 'amazing' series, and I never knew what they were talking about. Drove me nuts. So one summer, a couple of years ago—before Old Navy—I was bored beyond belief and read the first book in a day. Well, you know how that series is—you can't stop once you start, so I read the rest. It took about a week. Way too emotional and sappy, if you ask me. And believe me, guys would never act like that in real life. But it was funny to read. I laughed the whole way through, actually."

"It is *not* sappy. And it's not funny. And you know what? If guys acted more like Edward, they'd have a lot more real relationships."

He snorted. "Real relationships? With a vampire? Are you out of your mind?"

You know, I was getting really sick of hearing that question. "No. For your infor—"

My phone chimed, announcing a text. It was on the dresser right next to Jaden.

Dang. I smiled. "Can you hand me that, please?"

"What?" He looked surprised as he leaned over and snatched the phone. "Oh, you mean this?" He raised an eyebrow and held the cell phone up for me to see. "Are you sure you don't want me to read it for you?"

"Yes, I'm sure. Now hand it over," I said through gritted teeth.

"Hmm . . . I'm not sure it's safe for you to read this—especially with how mentally unstable you are right now. I think I should check it out for you first."

"Jaden. Give. Me. The. Phone." I was sitting up in bed, ready to spring at any moment.

He mockingly turned the screen on. The phone chimed again. "Oh, look. Two messages. And they're both from Tony.

Hmm . . . Now that just raised the stakes a bit, didn't it? Who's Tony?"

"Jaden Black, if you do not give me my phone now, I'll make sure your lip bleeds."

He held his arms out wide. "Oh, you wanna come and give me another kiss. I understand you can't bear to be apart from me."

"Ahhh!" I jumped out of bed. All teasing was gone.

Jaden was on his feet in a flash, tossing me the phone. "Here. Take it. Don't kill me!"

He laughed when it slipped through my fingers and I had to fumble to pick it up.

"Ha ha." I faked a smile and scrolled through the texts.

"So, is Tony your boyfriend?" Jaden asked as I climbed back on my bed to read.

"Hmm . . . ?" Already my mind was far away.

> thnking bout u 2day. wishd u
> couldve come. fun game. missd u.

"Wow! Look at you smile as you read that," Jaden said with a frown. "He is your boyfriend, isn't he?"

I looked up. "Tony?" I grinned like a fool and then blushed because of it. "No, he's not my boyfriend." I opened the next text.

> srry ths may sound crzy but u
> ok? i got a funy vibe earlier. was
> wondring if something hppnd?

Is he for real?

"What? What happened?" Jaden crossed over to me. "Why are you making a weird face?"

"Oh, it's nothing." I waved him away. *Just my vampire checking in on me. How cute is he?* I quickly texted back my reply.

> evrything fine. was a bit ruff earlier
> but im good now ur here.

"I have to wonder if that's what you looked like when you read my texts last night." Jaden looked down ruefully at me. "I blew it today, didn't I?" His voice had gone so soft, I almost didn't hear him.

I pushed "send" and put the phone down. He seemed like he really wanted to know.

"Look, Jaden, truthfully? Yes. You blew it." I sighed. "Girls don't like to be scared. Guys do. And we're all at different levels of scared toleration. The problem is, you hit my level. It wasn't funny. So much so, I probably won't go anywhere with you again. When you almost hit that kid, my heart left my body. I can't begin to imagine what would've happened if you had run over him. And frankly, I don't want to be anywhere near you when you *do* hit someone. You're a nice guy—more werewolf than guy, actually." I smiled slightly. "But nice. I just can't think of you the same way I did yesterday. I don't think I ever will."

Jaden sat down on the edge of Cassidy's bed and stared at the wall for a minute before lowering his head and nodding. "I can see where you're coming from." He rubbed his hands on his knees as he released a swoosh of air through his teeth.

My phone chimed again, announcing Tony's reply. I ignored it.

"Hey, I'm only here for the summer anyway. It's not like we'd ever see each other again, right?" I tried to make a joke, but I don't think it worked.

Jaden stared straight ahead. "I would've lost it, had my

sister driven with a guy like me," he muttered. "Kind of changes things when you put it in that perspective, doesn't it?"

I was so surprised, I didn't know what to say. "Jaden?"

He stood up and walked over to me. Very gently, he raised his hand and brushed a strand of hair from my forehead. "I'm not going to give up." He sighed. "There's something about you that's so different from other girls. Something alive—I don't know. You just see the world differently, I guess. It's kind of addicting, actually."

"Really?" I smiled a soft, slow smile. *Okay, so he was a total jerk, but under that, he was really sweet.*

"Goodbye, Claire Hart." He leaned forward like he was going to kiss me again. I didn't move. "I'm gonna kiss your forehead. Is that okay?" His eyes were full of mischief. "I just want to make sure you don't go for my throat with those teeth of yours before I can kiss you."

I grinned in response. "I can't promise anything—I mean, I am mentally unstable right now."

Jaden threw his head back and laughed. "Dang, Claire. Why'd I have to go and ruin everything, eh?"

I bit my lip, not sure how to answer.

He looked me right in the eye. "I know it's a long shot, but I'm going to try to win you back anyway. Just promise me you'll warn me next time you plan bodily damage."

My eyes lowered to his swollen lip, and I winced. *It* was *bad.* "Deal."

He chuckled. "Yep. It hurts." He leaned in, kissed me on the forehead, and whispered, "'Night, Claire. I'll call you in the morning."

"Bye."

I watched as he quietly left, and wondered why my heart felt as heavy as it did.

THIRTEEN

NEW LEAF, NEW MOON

"Okay, Mom. She's right here," Cassidy called through the door Jaden had just closed. A moment later, she opened it and waltzed in. "Yes, she looks fine. Yes, she's awake. Yep, she wants to talk to you. Her eager hands are waving in front of her face, begging me for the phone."

I rolled my eyes and pulled my hands out from under the covers. Mockingly, I begged for the phone. Cassidy smiled.

"Okay. Love you too. Buh-bye." She handed over the cell and whispered, "Don't blow it."

Like I planned to. Give me some credit. "Hi, Mom!" My voice was as happy as I could make it.

"Wow. So you fainted, huh? Were you embarrassed? Tell me everything that happened."

I didn't faint. "Look, Mom, it was no big deal, honest. Everyone else is freaking out, but I'm fine. Seriously. I could totally run the Boston Marathon tomorrow if I needed to." *Okay, so not the Boston Marathon—well, not any marathon, actually, but that was beside the point.*

"Really?" She didn't sound convinced.

I sighed. "Yes, Mom, really. I didn't eat much at lunch, and I guess I had forgotten to eat breakfast earlier, and Jaden and I were supposed to eat dinner at the game, so maybe once the heat hit me . . ." I trailed off, letting her fill in the pieces herself. "Anyway, I was stupid. I promise I'm not going to do it again."

My mom paused a moment, obviously processing that information. She was really good at reading between the lines. I knew she knew I was embarrassed and didn't want to make a big deal out of it. I also knew her main concern right then was the cause—and to make sure it didn't happen again. I waited.

"You know, your dad and I really like Jaden. He seems like a great guy."

They would.

"He did tell us you seemed overly tired. Aren't you sleeping enough?"

I'm sleeping fine. "I don't know. Maybe."

"What's Jaden look like?"

"Mo–om. He's not my boyfriend."

"Yeah, but you almost went on a date with him. He sounds cute. Cassidy says he's cute, Darlene says he's cute, but I want to know what *you* think."

He looks like a wolf to me. I'm not attracted to wolves. "He's cute, I guess. If you like guys who are tall, with dark hair, dark skin, and dark eyes, then he's perfect."

"Tall, dark, and mysterious?" She giggled.

I rolled my eyes again. "Mom, you read way too many books."

She laughed. "Look who's talking!"

I decided to ignore her. "I promise Jaden isn't anyone special, okay?" *So, let's just drop it.*

"Oh, so you must like the other guy better, then? Cass was telling me all about him."

"Cass?" I looked up and glared at her. She wasn't paying attention. She had *New Moon* open on her bed and was already reading. "She was, huh?" I leaned over and thunked her bed with my hand. She waved back at me but kept reading. "Yeah, well, he's nice. You'd like him."

"Which reminds me." Mom chuckled. "Since your father and I aren't there to do the Dating Ritual, I told Darlene my backup plan, in case we were ever away from you girls and you went on dates."

You've got to be kidding me. "You have a backup plan?" I'd forgotten all about the Dating Ritual—my parents' odd way of making sure guys were good enough to date their daughters. It was funny to watch my older sisters go through it, but me? That was a different story. All of a sudden, it didn't seem funny anymore. I closed my eyes and rubbed my hand over my face. "So, what's your backup plan?"

"Nope. It's a surprise! You'll just have to wait and see."

I groaned. *Mom is* way *too excited about this.*

"You know, missy, you should be very grateful that your parents love you enough to care about who you date."

Love me? Sure, if love is like mortifying and harassing your date until he never comes back. "I'm grateful," I muttered. "Really grateful." *Now, can I just go die somewhere, please?*

Mom laughed again. "You know you'll thank me when you're older."

"Why do you always say that?"

"Because it's true! Now be a good girl for Darlene, okay?"

Sheesh. Nothing like making me feel like I'm ten. "I am."

"Promise me that you and Cassidy are helping around the house, too. Oh, and you let me know if your sister isn't cleaning that room."

I smiled evilly and looked around the place. It was pretty much clean. "We are helping. And yeah, she's picking up after herself." My sister looked up and gave me a confused look. "But I promise to tell you the second Cassidy messes things up." She made a face at me and then started reading again.

"Okay." Mom sighed. "Don't forget to say your prayers. Miss you girls like crazy. Everything's quiet over here."

"Miss you too, Mom. And I promise to say my prayers. I love you. Tell Daddy I said hi."

"I will. Love you too, honey. Good night."

By Saturday, I'd almost forgiven Jaden—almost. At least, I'd forgotten to think about him and get angry again, which was just as good. Tony looked as cute as he could get in his coaching uniform when he picked me up to head to his YMCA soccer game.

"Are you ready to go?" He smiled at me from the living room. I'd just come down the stairs.

"Sure. Let me get my stuff." I walked over to the hall closet and pulled out my super-cute pink baseball cap and tossed it over my long braid. I slipped my cell in my back pocket, then grabbed a few dollars and my lip gloss out of my purse. I shoved them in my front pocket and turned around. "Okay, ready. Let's go."

"Wait! Wait!" Darlene exclaimed as she huffed her way down the stairs, still in her lounge pants and comfy shirt.

"What's wrong?" I paused on my way over to Tony. "Do you need me?"

"You?" Darlene laughed as she approached the bottom step.

"Oh, no! I don't need you. I need Tony."

"Me?" Tony looked surprised. "Sure—uh, what can I help you with?"

Darlene grinned a Cheshire cat grin and said, "Just a sec," before she turned around and hollered up the stairs, "Roger! Are you coming? These two need to go, so if you're going to be here to watch this, then you've got to come now."

What in the world is she—? And then it hit me like a ton of bricks. *The Dating Ritual! Dang.* "Uh, look, Darlene. Tony and I are just friends." I hurried over to her. "Honest. I'm sure my mom wouldn't even consider this a date. I'm positive, actually. So, you really don't have to worry about it." I turned to Tony for support. He gave me a funny look. "Right, Tony?" I asked, nodding my head slightly in Darlene's direction. "This isn't a *date*, right?"

"Uh . . ." Obviously, he wasn't sure what his script was. I saw that panicked look in his eyes, and I knew it meant trouble. He improvised. "Some people may call going and watching a game a date, but I . . . uh . . ." He glanced back at me. "I don't?"

I smiled. "Of course you don't!" Turning back to Darlene, I gushed, "See, everything's fine! Thanks so much for thinking of us. We're going to go." I stepped up to her and gave her a hug. "You're the best."

Just as I was making my escape, Roger came pounding down the stairs. "Okay, I'm here. Go ahead—you can do it now." He looked so excited, you'd have thought it was Christmas.

"Well, I'm sorry, Claire," Darlene was saying. "I still consider this a date, and your mom did say . . ."

That's it. I'm so going to kill my mom.

"So, Tony, if you'd come here, please?" Darlene was all giddiness.

"Sure." Tony gave me a confused look as he made his way

over to her. Roger was standing right next to Darlene and even reached out to give Tony a friendly pat on the shoulder.

The poor guy. What are they going to do to him?

It was like watching a wreck. You want to look away, but you can't. Instead, you stare in horror.

Darlene began her speech. I could tell she'd been practicing.

"So, Tony. I don't know if Claire's told you, but her family puts all their daughters' dates through sort of a test to see if they can date them, you know? They call it a Dating Ritual. And since Claire's mom isn't around, she asked me to fill in for her."

"Okay." Tony looked a little scared. "So, uh, you're going to make me do something?"

Darlene laughed. "Yep. Stand right next to me." Tony took a few steps forward and stopped about three feet from her. "Nope. A little closer than that." She motioned forward again, and Roger snorted with laughter.

We all looked over at his outburst. Darlene dug him in the ribs with her elbow and pasted a smile on her face. "Come here, Tony. Stand right here."

With a wary glance in my direction, Tony took another step toward her and stopped. "Is this good?"

What in the heck did my mom tell her to do?

All at once, Darlene's hand snaked out and grabbed Tony by the ear. She pulled him right up to her mouth and whispered loudly enough for all of us to hear, "Claire was a virgin when she left this house, and by golly she'll be a virgin when she comes home. You got that?"

WHAT? "No!" I squeaked before covering my mouth and turning every color on the palette. *Why me? Why me? Why me?*

Roger burst into large guffaws, and Darlene giggled girlishly.

I'd never seen anyone look as truly shocked or as mortified as Tony, but of course, I didn't have a mirror. He stammered and nodded while trying to disengage himself from Darlene's grasp. "Y–y–yes, Mrs. Hadley! I promise not to touch her!"

I hate my family. I hate my family's friends. Seriously, life is not meant to be this hard. Poor Tony, too. He'd never even kissed a girl. Now, Jaden I could understand, but Tony?

Roger laughed all the louder. Darlene smothered a small chuckle herself and finally released Tony, saying simply, "Okay then, you two run along and have a great time. Let us know who wins." She waved a happy little hand at us.

Tony wasted no time. He refused to even look at me as he turned around, his face bright red. He grabbed my hand and maneuvered us out the door and down the steps in two seconds flat.

The car ride was a bit uncomfortable as well. I could tell he was still mortified, especially when he asked, "So, um, does that mean your mom thinks—I mean, did she make Darlene do that because they all think I'd—?"

"No! Honestly." *Oh my gosh.* I turned around and faced him. "Um, I'm sorry. I had no idea what they were going to do. They do randomly weird, embarrassing things to all the guys. You have to believe me—I'm just as freaked out as you are. Except, I mean, I *did* know my family was crazy, so maybe you are more freaked out than I am."

"I can believe your family is crazy." Tony glanced over at me. I could see he was trying not to laugh.

I smiled. "Actually, you may have gotten off easier than what my mom and dad would have done to you. Darlene's not quite as good as my mom. She would've probably scared the living daylights—"

"Oh, don't get me wrong. I'm scared. Really scared. Believe

me, that . . . uh . . . is a very effective Dating Ritual thingy. At least, I don't think you'll have any problems with, uh . . ." His face grew bright red, and so did mine. He jerked his attention back to the road.

I decided to change the subject, but my mind went blank. All I could think about was that stupid virgin threat. *Okay, think of something. Anything.* I cleared my throat. "So, your game. How old are the kids on the team?"

Tony smiled, looking relieved. "They're mostly six and seven."

"Six and seven? Oh my gosh. How cute is that? You coach first graders?"

Tony nodded his head and chuckled. "They're really cool, too. Some of those little guys can run almost as fast as me."

Aw. I could just picture him running on the field with them. From his expression, I could tell he really loved coaching them. "So, what's your team's name?"

Tony glanced down and shook his head. "I didn't come up with it, believe me. The whole team had a say, and I got outvoted." He laughed. "We're the Bumble Bees."

FOURTEEN ♥ A PERFECT DAY

"The Bumble Bees? As in bzzz bzzz?"

"Yeah." He snorted and then imitated a little kid's voice. "'It's cuz we have gots a stinger, and stingers hurts.'"

"Didn't you tell them that once a bee stings someone, it dies?"

"Ah, man. I should've thought of that. Where were you when I needed you?"

I chuckled. "So, what team are you playing against?"

"Uh, today that would be the Fighting Ninja Warriors."

I burst into laughter.

"Yeah, I'm totally expecting to get our butts kicked." He laughed with me. "Something tells me Fighting Ninja Warriors aren't afraid of little Bumble Bees."

"Ya think?" I giggled again. I couldn't help it.

"You want to know the worst part?" His eyes playfully sparkled into mine for a second.

"There's more?"

"Yep." He nodded and focused back on the road. "Our uniforms are purple."

"Purple bees?" I bit back a grin. "Purple bees can be cute."

"Yeah, if you're a Care Bear, maybe."

That was it—I lost it. I totally cracked up all over again. Tony was seriously so cute. He kept me giggling the whole way to the soccer field. It was amazing, the direct contrast between him and Jaden.

I should've never gone out with that wolf! If I hadn't, I could've already seen the Bumble Bees play. Besides, who wouldn't love to hang out with a vampire all day? Especially if he was as cute as Tony.

Since he was the assistant coach and expected to be early, we were the first ones on the field. I unloaded the cones while he hauled out the big net of balls he had stashed in his trunk. It only took a few moments to get the cones set out and the soccer balls freed and lined up for the children.

He was teaching me a few dribbling tricks with the ball when the kids started to show up. He was super good—his feet were so quick and light, by the time my feet would make it to where I'd seen the ball, it was already gone. I really didn't want to stop, but the kids had other ideas. They were way too excited to see Tony.

As they came on the field, they raced right over and started ganging up on him, each little guy eager to be the one who stripped the ball from him. Tony laughed and ran all over the field, barely keeping the ball in front, with loads of kids chasing from behind. It was easy to see that this was a warm-up game he played with them all the time. Everyone was laughing, and some of the parents egged the kids on.

"Come on, Max! Get 'im! Get Mr. Tony."

"Kayla! The other way! Go the other way! Look, Mr. Tony's

comin' up behind you!"

"Go, Justin! You can do it! Get the ball from Mr. Tony!"

I decided it was my turn. "Run, Mr. Tony! Run!" I shouted loud enough to be heard over the parents' laughter and shouts as I climbed up to sit on the bleachers.

Tony must've heard me because he whipped his head up and smiled the cutest smile I'd ever seen just before a little girl rammed right into him, causing him to trip over the ball and go sprawling onto the field.

Oops.

It became a mad chaos of chuckles and whoops as the kids all tackled him in one large, purple dog pile.

Tony finally emerged the winner, smiling triumphantly with the ball in his hand and children dripping from him. It was the most charming thing I'd ever seen. My heart practically burst from my chest with happiness.

Is there a more perfect guy on the planet? No way—it has to be him. Eeeh! And he's smiling right at me.

It became all seriousness once the coach arrived and blew his whistle. The children and Tony jumped to attention immediately and jogged over to the man, who looked like he was in his early forties. Within seconds, the team was back on the field, and Tony was leading them through a series of proper warm-ups. Even that was fun to watch.

Of course, it helped that every few minutes Tony would look up from what he was doing and grin at me.

Just before the game started, it was discovered that they were short a referee, so Tony quickly volunteered. He grabbed a black referee shirt and ran across the field up to the stand where I was sitting.

"Hey, can you hold this?" he asked, not even slightly winded. He looked up at me mischievously.

I bit my lip and stared down at him. *He is so hot.* "Hold what?"

"This."

Before I could blink, Tony leaned forward and whisked off his shirt right in front of me. *Oh!* I glanced away as he pulled the other one over his head.

"Thanks," he replied. He flung the shirt in my lap and climbed up the side of the bleachers, giving me a swift kiss on the cheek before dashing back out to the field again.

My hand flew to my cheek, while my other one clasped the white coach uniform. I didn't care that it was slightly damp—he'd just been wearing it! Once he made it out to the field again, he ran backward a few steps and gave me a wink and a little salute, then focused solely on the game about to begin.

There was something almost magical about that game. Even though the Bumble Bees lost, they didn't seem upset or disappointed. In fact, every one of the little guys got a special hug and a high-five from Tony at the end. He also made it a point to exclaim in the coolest, older-brother voice I'd ever heard, "Man, you rocked! You are the best soccer player in the whole world!" Every kid heard the same thing. And they knew he told them all the same thing—they were all standing right there—but they didn't care. They knew they were special and that Tony loved them. I could tell that was all that mattered.

I'd never seen so many happy, excited kids run home after losing a game, but it made me think, *really* think. *Just who are you, Tony Russo? How can one guy capture the hearts of so many people around him? And does your heart have room for one more?* All at once, I wanted to be a part of his life—that is, if he'd let me.

{♥}

When I got home, Darlene announced that we'd all been invited to the Russos' for a get-together Tuesday evening. My heart flip-flopped when she said the words. I couldn't believe we'd been invited to Tony's house. *His house.* Just like when Bella was invited over to Edward's home for the first time. I couldn't wait to see what it looked like inside.

Tuesday couldn't come fast enough for me. When it did, I was just so darned excited that nothing could've stopped me from going. Nothing.

Just as I finished putting on my makeup, I got a text. I thought it might've been Tony because we had been texting on and off all day. I opened it and was surprised to see it was from Jaden.

> hey think we should go 2 the movie
> 2nite. what u say?

Yeah, right. Not on your life.

> sorry I have plans already :oP

Jaden was undaunted.

> why dont U cancel them?

> cant but thx 4 asking.

It wasn't thirty minutes later when the wolf came to the door, holding two movie tickets. "Hi. I thought if you saw the tickets, you wouldn't be able to say no."

Darlene came to the door just as I answered him. "Look, Jaden, I'm sorry you bought them already, but I told you I'm going somewhere else. I can't."

"Wait a minute." Darlene leaned over my shoulder and tugged the tickets out of Jaden's hand. "Hey, this looks like a good movie. You don't have to go to the Russos' house if you don't want to."

"I want to." My smile tightened.

"I'm sure they'd be fine if you went with Jaden. Besides, you can't waste these." Darlene held the tickets in front of my face.

Jaden went in for the kill. "Yeah. You don't want me to waste them, do you?"

I would've smacked the smug look off his face if Darlene hadn't been standing right there. Instead, I heaved an exasperated sigh. "Look, I know you spent money, but I did text you and say I wasn't coming. I can't just bail on my friends. Sorry."

"Oh, go with Jaden, Claire. I'm sure it'll be more fun watching a movie than hanging out with us old folks, anyway."

"Exactly. Looks like you're leaving with me."

"Come on, out you go." Darlene began to nudge me out the door. "I'll tell the Russos what happened. I'm sure they'll understand. And don't worry about the Dating Ritual thingy—we already know Jaden's a good guy."

I could see my hopes and dreams of spending time with Tony vanish in a puff of smoke. "No. I'm not going—the Russos won't understand. Besides, Jaden's not as good as you think." I dug in my heels just as he leaned in and swung one arm around my waist. I was no match for his strength. In less than a second I found myself heading toward his car as he hollered out behind him, "Thanks, Darlene. I'll bring her back safe and sound."

"Jaden, stop!" I pushed against him, and to my surprise, he let me go.

"What?"

"I'm not going with you."

"But— "

"No." I folded my arms and glared, daring him to challenge me again.

"You've gotta be kidding me. You're still mad about the other day? Seriously?"

"Yes, I am, but this has nothing to do with it. The issue here is I've told you repeatedly I'm going somewhere, and you still expect me to drop everything and run off with you."

"So, what's the big deal? It's just a boring dinner, right? Wouldn't you rather go see a movie?"

Why is it so hard to talk to this guy? "It wouldn't matter if you were taking me to Paris—I still wouldn't miss this dinner. You know why? Because they asked me first. Period. End of discussion."

"So, I just spent money on these tickets, and you won't go, even though Darlene says you can?"

"Yep."

"That's just stupid."

"No, standing here debating with you is stupid." I spun around and stomped up to the house. Jaden was hot on my heels.

"Come on, Claire. You're just being immature. I don't know why I even bothered coming here in the first place."

Grr. "Neither do I!" I didn't realize Darlene was still standing at the door until I looked up as I came toward it. She quickly scuttled out of the way. "I'm staying here," I announced to them both, just to be clear. Once I entered, I turned and put a hand up to stop Jaden from coming in. "Thank you for inviting me. Now go find someone else to take." I plastered a smile on my face to placate Darlene's shocked gasp. "Look, you're a nice guy. Just listen to what I say next time, okay?"

He rested a hand on the doorframe and shook his head like he couldn't believe I was actually turning him down. "Fine. Whatever. I hope you have fun." With a sneer, he pushed himself away.

I hardened my heart against the nagging self-pressure that insisted I was wrong as he walked back to his car. I was right. I *knew* I was right. It was the principle of the matter.

It was also the first time I had ever been faced with opposition, done what I wanted to do, and really stuck with it. I glanced over at Darlene. She wasn't happy with me. Thank goodness she didn't say anything, but by the way she was biting her lip, I knew I had gone down a few points in her book.

That hurt.

Jaden roaring the car to life and pulling out of the driveway hurt.

I don't like people to be mad at me. I straightened my shoulders and quickly climbed the stairs to my room, reminding myself as I did that I would've hurt Tony more if I hadn't stood my ground.

{♥}

Tony Russo was most definitely a vampire. I knew it as soon as we drove down the long, winding road that led to the large, many-windowed home.

Cassidy must've seen the look on my face, because she grabbed my hand and whispered, "Not one word about them being vampires. Do you hear me?"

"But look at the house," I whispered back, pointing to an almost exact replica of Edward Cullen's home. "Oh my gosh! It even has a huge garage." As soon as the car stopped, I jumped out of my seat and out the door.

Cassidy quickly followed suit. "Claire. Okay, I know you think this looks like the Cullens' house, but really, you—"

Just then the door opened, and my heart stopped at the sight of Tony bounding down the steps to greet us. His casual, white button-down shirt matched his bright smile. In less than two seconds he was at my side.

"You made it." His eyes looked mischievously into mine. "Come on." He gently tugged on my hand. "I have a surprise for you."

FIFTEEN
♥
DÈJÁ VU

"A surprise?" I couldn't help it—I grinned back. *What in the world—?*

"Yeah, come in. You'll love it."

Cassidy's jaw dropped as we brushed past his parents, who were coming down to greet Darlene and Roger.

Just as Tony and I entered the house, Nora came up to us. "So, have you told her about the surprise yet? Come on in, Cassidy. You can hang out with me. These two are going to be busy for a bit."

Oh my gosh. My heart began to pound.

"Thanks," Tony whispered.

"Just hurry up before Mom and Dad notice you're gone."

Tony didn't need any more encouragement. We were through the main room and climbing the stairs before I'd even had a moment to comprehend that I was actually in his house. *In Tony's house. Eeeh!* "So, are we going to your room?" I didn't want to tell him my sister would freak out if she knew I was going to a guy's room, just he and I. Alone.

Tony paused on the top stair. "No. Your surprise is up here. My room's downstairs. I have a lot of stuff in there—in my room—so I don't usually show it to anyone."

My smile turned into a chuckle. "Are you saying your room is a mess?"

He bit his lip and looked away briefly. "Would you drop the subject if I said it was dirty? Would that make you never want to see it?" His gaze held mine.

"Never want to—?" *What does that mean?* "No, it'd make me want to see it more."

"Oh, then it's clean. It's the cleanest room you've ever seen."

Is he joking? I laughed. "Okay." *Now I'm dying to see it!* "What are you hiding in there?"

"Hiding?" Tony's face went white. He tugged on my hand and started walking again. "What do you mean, hiding? I'm not hiding anything."

I had never heard anyone sound guiltier in my life. *Yeah, right.* "Good try."

We wound down a hallway into a large loft area. Tony remained silent.

"You're really not going to tell me what's in your room?"

"Look." He stopped and pushed his hair out of his eyes. "There *is* something about me that I'd love to share with you—but I can't right now. My parents would lose it if I did. As soon you as walked in my room, you'd realize what I can't tell you. It's pretty obvious."

Duh! He's a vampire. He's probably stressing because he doesn't have a bed in his room. I'm such an idiot.

All of a sudden, I had an urge to tell him not to worry because I already knew who he was. It was ridiculous to keep hiding something so obvious, anyway. But just as I opened my mouth, he spoke first.

"Okay, so are you ready for your surprise?" Tony dropped my hand, walked over to the stereo on the far wall and rummaged around a bit, and then quickly shoved something behind his back.

He was the most adorable guy on the planet when he walked up to me. His smile was beyond contagious. *What is he doing?* By the time he stood right in front of me, my heart was beating at warp speed. I couldn't say anything even if I wanted to.

"So, Nora says that you love the Twilight books."

"Twilight?" *Oh my gosh! Is he going to say it?*

"And that you're a big fan of the movie as well."

"Yeah?"

"Well, I have something for you."

"Okay." *Spill.*

"It's nothing major. Just, sometimes I get the opportunity to meet some cool people, and, well, I ran into this band, and they—"

"Band?" I wasn't following.

"Yeah, I'm sure you've heard of them before. Anyway, they gave me a couple of signed copies of their CD, so I was wondering if you wanted one." Tony pulled a Paramour CD from behind his back and gave it to me.

"No way!"

"I know it's not their new album, but I thought you'd like it anyway, since it has songs from the original *Twilight* movie on it."

Holy cow! "Like it? Tony, this is awesome! I love it!" I flipped it over in my hands. It was signed by every person in the band. "But are you sure you want to give this to me? It's probably worth something—"

Tony shook his head. "It's only worth what someone will pay for it. And I have a strong suspicion you'd pay a lot more for it than I would."

"Yeah, but—"

"Keep it. I have enough CDs to last me a lifetime or more."

I was so blown over by his generosity, I didn't know what to say except thank you. I let my smile say the rest of what I couldn't.

Tony liked the smile—I could tell by the way he watched me. I thought he might try to kiss me again, but all at once he cleared his throat and straightened. "Look, we should go so my parents don't get worried."

Oh. Darn. My smile went taut, and I fidgeted with the CD. "Yeah, you're probably right. I'm sure Darlene and Roger would be worried too." I knew they wouldn't be—they probably didn't even know I was missing, but I had to say something.

"And Claire?"

"Yeah?"

"Just know that if I could tell you something about me right now, I would. But I can't. Maybe one day we can get this whole thing sorted out, but for now, could you be patient?"

"Yes." *Besides, I already know what your secret is.*

For the next three weeks, Tony took me all over Seattle and taught me what it was like to be a true Seattleite. I could see why he loved the place as he did. It was so beautiful! I'd never laughed so much or done so much in so little time as I did with him. Each day was a new adventure through the eyes of my very own vampire. Every night he'd send me a series of texts about the silly things that had happened that day, making me giggle. He never tried to kiss me, so I pretty much stopped worrying about that first kiss. Deep down inside, I really wanted him to, but for now, I could just relax and be myself around him.

Then one day, it finally happened.

When Nora called to invite me to go with her to the discount mall for the second time, I was hesitant to see Jaden again until . . . .

"Tony said he'd drive us, if we wanted to go," Nora announced proudly through my cell.

"Tony? Really? He wants to come with us to *that* mall?"

"I know—like, crazy, right? I mean, why would he want to head over there now, when all this time he's been avoiding the place like it was Volterra or something?"

Volterra? My head snapped up and I almost dropped the phone. "What do you mean?" *I can't believe she just mentioned the home of the most dangerous vampire clan in the Twilight series. Was she trying to tell me something?*

"You do know who the Volturi are, right?"

"Of course I do. What girl doesn't?"

"Oh, okay. You had me worried for a second there."

"No—I mean, why did you compare the mall to Volterra? I don't understand. Was it for a reason?"

Nora chuckled. "I use it all the time, actually. It makes a real good line."

"Oh."

"So, are you coming or what? Tony says to see if eleven is okay."

"Yeah, eleven's fine. I'll see you then."

"Okay, bye."

"Where are you going?" Cassidy looked up from reading my book as I hung up the phone. She was sprawled out in the middle of the bed again.

I shrugged. "Just to the mall. Do you want to come?"

"Um, no. Can't."

"Why?" I walked over to the dresser and pulled out my makeup case.

"Why? Um, because no thanks to a certain vampire/werewolf-loving freak in this room, I have to read this whole series. Hello? Why didn't you tell me these were the most addicting books on the planet?"

"I did." I smirked and tossed my makeup case on the bed before opening the closet to find another shirt. "You just didn't listen to me."

"Ugh!" Cassidy threw herself back on the bed and brought the book up to her eye level. "Is she ever going to be a vampire? Ever? Just answer me that much, please? It's driving me crazy."

I shuffled through a few shirts. "You'll just have to read to find out."

"You're evil, you know that? Really evil."

Laughing, I pulled out a pretty red shirt with a big sparkly heart across the front. "Thanks. It's a tough job, but somebody's gotta do it." I snatched up my case and sprinted to the bathroom, barely missing the pillow Cassidy tossed just before the door closed.

"So this is the hallowed mall—the mall of malls, huh?" Tony asked with a skeptical look. "Doesn't seem that great to me." He shrugged when Nora threw a withering glance in his direction. "What?" He looked so completely boyish and adorable, I forgave him immediately.

"You know, buddy, you aren't as smart as you seem to be," she huffed. "Anyone with half a brain would know an amazing place the second they saw it." She pushed past him and kept walking.

"Maybe that's my problem then," he retorted behind her. "I've got a whole brain, not half of one."

I smothered a snort and glared at Tony when he turned to gauge my reaction.

"All right, I give." He shook his head and held his hand out for me. "You girls win. This is the best mall in the whole universe."

I ignored his hand and hitched my purse up onto my shoulder again. With my head raised, I walked past him too. "You know, I would actually believe you if your voice had some enthusiasm in it."

"Come on—guys aren't supposed to love malls. It's like a rule or something," he protested as he caught up to me. I was trying to get to Nora, who was still beating a path to Old Navy. "You have to admit that."

I looked over at him, and my heart stopped. Both his hands were in his pockets, and a thatch of light brown hair had fallen across his brow. He looked so cute, I'd almost forgotten what we were talking about.

"What?" He smiled at me as we hurried through the large court.

Dang, he's hot! Like really, really hot! "I was—oh!" I ran into the back of a large woman. Her weight was the only thing that kept us both up, barely.

"Hey!" she yelled. "Watch where you're going!"

"I'm so sorry! Are you all right?"

When she turned around, I felt even worse. Sitting in front of her was a toddler in a stroller she'd been pushing. *Yikes!*

"Is he all right? I'm really sorry. I didn't mean—please forgive me—"

"You know, it's punks like you that make it really hard to shop in malls!" She was obviously very upset.

People were staring. I couldn't even look at Tony.

"I'm sorry. I know, it was my fault—"

"You better be sorry!" she snarled. "Now do me a favor and watch where you're going."

"Look." Tony's deep voice near my ear startled me. "Is there any way we can repay you? We're really sorry. And a lot of it is my fault. I was talking to Claire, and she wasn't—"

"Looking where she was going?" The woman finished, her arms folded across her large torso. "Really, genius? It's nice to know you figured that out."

I was surprised to see Tony smile. "Thanks. But seriously, an ice cream cone for the little guy, or something? Please, let us make it up to you."

I felt his arm wrap around my waist and pull me next to him, almost as if he were protecting me. It worked. I felt very protected.

"What's going on?" Nora asked. She must've heard the yelling and come back to help.

"Wait a minute. Do I know you?" The woman asked. "You seem kind of familiar. Are you a movie star or something?"

Tony stepped back, pulling me with him. "Uh, star? No." His laughter sounded forced. "You must have me confused with someone else."

"Are you sure?" The woman seemed uncertain for a moment, and then she pointed her finger at him. "No, no. I'm positive, now that I think about it. I've seen you somewhere before."

Oh my gosh!

People all around us began to whisper. I heard a few gasps.

Tony was freaking out. I had never seen him so pale before. "N–no, no. You've got me confused with someone else. It happens all the time." His hands shook as he released me and whipped out his wallet. Nervously, he rummaged through it until he came up with a few bills. "Here, have lunch on me. So sorry about the accident." He crushed the money into her palm, and with a little wave said, "Hope you have a good day." His arm wrapped around my waist again, and he maneuvered us out of the area so quickly I thought his feet would catch on fire.

SIXTEEN
♥
DANGEROUS SECRETS

Nora had to run to catch up to us. "Dang!" She panted. "Why does that always happen to you?"

"Drop it, Nora." Tony's voice was clipped as he moved faster. I very nearly had to fly to keep up. Not that it was hard—with his arm around me in a vice grip, I didn't have much choice.

She wasn't going to be put off that easily. "You know Mom and Dad said you aren't supposed to make scenes. If you just acted like everyone else, no one would notice you. What'd you do, anyway? Why were you talking to her?"

"Nora, stop it. Please."

"Yeah, but you know better. You hardly ever talk to people when we're out. What happened?"

Tony halted to a stop and jerked around, facing her. "It was nothing, okay?" He flicked his eyes in my direction, and then back over to her. "Just an accident. Now leave it, all right? I don't want to discuss anything right *now.*"

Nora's eyes were huge as she looked over at me attached to

his hip. "Oh. Sorry."

What in the world is going on? Just who is Tony Russo, anyway? Is there something besides him being a vampire that I don't know about?

He grunted and ran his free hand through his hair. "Great. Thanks. Nothing like keeping 'you know what' under wraps." He glanced over at me again and then sort of half smiled as he released his hold a bit on my waist. "Claire, I . . ." He heaved a sigh and closed his eyes a minute, agitation written all over his face. It was obvious that whatever was going on, he didn't want me to know about it. He took another breath and started again. "Claire, there's some—"

"Tony, stop." I pulled away from him completely. "It's no big deal. You don't have to tell me anything anyway." My fingers fiddled with the strap of my purse as I hitched it higher. He still looked upset. I smiled.

"Claire, there's—it's just—"

"Don't worry about it." I turned around so he wouldn't see the hurt in my eyes. Not that he needed to tell me anything. I mean, I wasn't his girlfriend or whatever—it's just, I was hurt anyway, with no reason to explain it. "It's obvious there's something going on that you want to hide, but no worries. It's no big deal if you don't want to tell me."

"Claire, I *can't* tell you." He stepped up next to me and put his arm across my shoulders. "There's a difference."

My eyes met his a moment before looking away. "Yeah, it's no big deal." I smiled again. "So, who's ready for Old Navy?"

"Claire," he growled.

What is it with guys growling at me lately? I met his eyes again. He was staring right at me, almost as if he were trying to tell me something. *What, vampire? All of a sudden,* now *you want to talk to me? Well, then, spit it out.* His gaze was so intense my heart stopped beating right then and there, completely belying my cool façade. *Oh my gosh! He can probably see right past all this anyway, can't he? Can he tell how much I'm really starting to like him? Like, borderline-unhealthy-crazed sort of starting to like him? Holy cow! I'm already a groupie, and I don't even know who he is!*

"Oh, just tell her," Nora exclaimed.

"I can't." He was still looking at me.

Why not? I gulped.

"You know it'll break my contract if I do."

Contract? Curiosity was killing me.

"You know, for a guy who's been obsessing about Claire all this time, you're sure sending out all the wrong signals if you want her to think you're interested." His twin smiled annoyingly at us both.

I could cheerfully kill her.

Tony's eyes went cold. "Thanks, Nora. I owe you one."

The underlying threat behind his words must've hit home. "Aw, come on, Tony. Give me a break—I'm only teasing you. Besides, I never thought I'd say it, but I hope you actually succeed with this one." With that, she turned around and started walking back the way we'd come.

"Where you going?" he called after her.

She glanced back and smirked. "Uh, hate to break it to you, but Old Navy's this way. You *are* coming, right, Claire?"

"Yeah. Of course."

"Good." Her smile was icky sweet. "I think Tony needs to see his competition face to face. It'll be good for him to know he actually has to win a girl's heart this time." Nora turned and laughed as she marched forward.

Oh, no. I'd almost forgotten about Jaden. I really, really didn't want to go to Old Navy.

"Uh, look." I glanced back up at Tony. "If you'd rather stay here and not go through those people again—I mean, hide out a bit, I don't mind waiting with you."

His eyes scanned my face, and he smothered a chuckle. "Yeah, Nora can be scary sometimes. Believe me, I know. I've lived with her the last seventeen years."

It wasn't really his sister I was worried about. "You know, I—uh, think I caught that vibe, actually."

"You did?" His smile nearly blew me away. But it was the way his eyes probed mine that did the most damage to my well-being. "Thank you."

I scrunched my forehead. "For?"

"For being so great about everything." He heaved another sigh and looked around. "Look, I know you probably have a few questions."

More like a hundred thousand.

"But thanks for acting like you don't." His eyes seared into mine again. "This isn't easy for me. I'm not really a guy who tries to hide stuff—if you know what I mean. I'm just more like, what ya see is whatcha get."

"It's okay. I get it." I nodded my head and then grinned.

"What?" His mouth imitated mine. "What are you smiling for?"

"I don't know." I shrugged and briefly glanced down. I could feel a massive blush coming on, but I met his gaze despite it. "It makes you more mysterious in a way."

"Mysterious?" Tony absorbed that for a moment. "Ah! I'm a puzzle. So, you like solving things, do you?"

"I guess you could say that." *This flirting thing is getting way easier than I ever expected.*

"So, Nancy Drew," he teased as he put his arm around me again, "just how brave are you?"

Not at all. I'm a total wimp. "Oh, very brave."

"Then let's go meet this Jaden guy, eh?" He took a step forward. I didn't move a muscle. "You're not telling me that a girl who loves mysteries and solving puzzles is chicken, are you?"

Ugh. "Of course not. I was just fixing my purse." I brought it up to my shoulder and allowed Tony to bring me closer to his side. "Besides, I don't think it's me who has to worry about being brave."

"Touché!" He chuckled. "Bring it on."

The vampire meets the werewolf. All at once, I hoped Stephenie Meyer was wrong about them being archenemies. *I mean, really, can't we all just get along?*

{♥}

"Claire! I knew you'd come back." Jaden's deep voice startled me so much that I dropped the shirt I'd just pulled off the rack.

"Jaden? You *are* here."

"Of course I'm here." He looked at me like I'd gone nuts, and then he bent down to collect the shirt. "I work here, remember?"

I nervously glanced around—I couldn't see Tony anywhere. *Good.* "Yeah, uh, I know. I just couldn't find you when I came in, so I thought you weren't here for some reason."

"You were looking for me?" Jaden smirked wolfishly and moved a step closer.

Yikes. I stepped back. About ten hangers jabbed me from behind as I collided with the rack. "Well, um—not really. I was just going to say hi, is all."

"You know what I think?" He reached his arm around my

shoulder and hung up the shirt. His arm stayed conveniently next to me as he shifted his weight against the rack. It was a strong rack.

"No." I eyed him warily. "I'd rather not know what you think. I'm still mad at you."

He chuckled and brought his free hand up to brush my hair away from my face. I was fast learning that was one of his favorite things to do—touch my hair. "Really? You better not tell me that. I think I like it when you're mad."

"You would." *Sheesh. This is all Tony needs to see right now.* I pushed against Jaden's chest and said forcefully, "Go away."

"Nope." His grin was overwhelmingly arrogant. "I'm not leaving until you admit that you really came here because you couldn't stop thinking about me."

"Are you for real?" I groaned and pushed against him again. "Go away and leave me alone, Jaden, before I kick your butt."

He looked down at my hands and laughed at my efforts. "I'd like to see you try."

"Really?" I was game if he was. "You really want to see me kick your butt?"

"Yeah." His eyes were still on my hands. I had the distinct impression he liked them against his chest.

I bit back my sudden annoyance and repulsion, and instead looked at him flirtatiously. "Are you sure? Because I'll do it right here and now."

"Go for it," he whispered huskily.

As I straightened my back and stepped closer to him, my eyes simmered into his. I allowed my hands to travel up and over his shoulders, and I bit my lip slightly as they traveled down the top of his arms and then back under to stroke the warm, sinewy muscles beneath his short-sleeved shirt. "Rule number one," I whispered temptingly. "When an annoying guy won't leave you alone, reach underneath his arms" —my hands glided slowly up underneath his arms— "grab a chunk of hair, and yank."

"OW!" Jaden jerked away, his hands protectively covering his underarms. "Holy cra—mother of a—sea lion's uncle! What was that? Are you trying to kill me, or what?" I saw tears spring to his eyes briefly before he turned his back on me and bounced a bit to shake out the pain.

"No. I'm kicking your butt, remember?" I said scornfully as Tony came running toward me.

"Claire, are you all right?" His concerned face was such a relief after Jaden's leer.

"Yeah, I'm fine."

"Is *she* all right?" Jaden whipped around. "Are you kidding, man? You're concerned about her?" He pointed at me with one of his elbows. "Are you out of your mind? That little spitfire is fine. Take my word for it."

"It's true." I smiled as I put my hands on my hips. "I'm fine. Just remember, you asked for it."

"Whatever!" Jaden pouted as he rubbed his underarms. "I said you could kick my butt, not maim me."

"You're such a baby, you know that?"

"Wait." Tony seemed a little off guard. "Are you Jaden?"

Jaden looked at him suspiciously before answering. "Yeah, that's my name. What's it to you?"

Tony took in his towering form. Jaden was seriously a big guy. "Nothing, just curious." He nodded his head before turning back to me. "So, he was bugging you, and you took him out?"

"You could say that." I glared at Jaden. *He's* always *bugging me.* Smiling tightly, I focused on Tony again. "Did you find something you like?" I asked, but what I meant was, "Are you ready to leave now? You met Jaden—let's go."

"Um, sure. I could get a couple things." Tony glanced at me and then back up at Jaden. "Do we just pay for it up front, or is there a cash register back here?"

"I'll take you up front," Jaden graciously offered. *Too graciously.* He rubbed his underarms a moment more, then led us to the checkout.

Actually, the whole meeting incident took place much more easily and more stress free than I'd thought it would. I don't know what I expected—maybe for them to duke it out or something—but it wasn't until the checkout that things got a little testy.

Jaden sulked a bit as he got the machine ready. When he turned to look at us, he watched Tony for a second, but refused to look at me. I watched a confused expression come over Jaden's face, and then hesitantly, he stepped back. Surveying Tony from a different angle, he picked up the shirts on the counter. "Don't I know you from someplace?" he asked as he scanned the first one. "I can't put my finger on it, but I'm sure I've met you before."

Oh my gosh. Not Jaden, too.

"Really?" Tony shrugged and acted cool, but kept his eyes averted from Jaden's. "Hmm . . . I don't know. Maybe."

"Nah, I'm pretty good with faces. I'll figure it out."

I wonder if he'll tell me once he figures it out.

"What's your name?" Jaden abruptly asked.

I jumped in. "Oh, this is Tony. Tony Russo."

Both guys looked at me.

Then all at once, it dawned on Jaden. "Ah, the guy texting you the other night. I remember now." He smiled smugly at Tony, but quickly replaced his smirk with a look of bafflement.

Did he have to imply we were together? I smiled. "Yep.

This is him."

"Tony?" Jaden appeared to mull that over as he scanned the other shirt. "Are you sure that's your name?"

Tony looked down at his hands, and I laughed. "Uh, yeah. I think he'd know his own name."

"Really? I don't know why, but you seem like a Jason, or John, or, or a Jack to me."

Tony stiffened. "That's funny. Not something you hear every day—someone questioning your name. Uh, what's the total?" It was obvious he wanted out of there.

Jaden told him the price, and Tony quickly brought out his wallet and paid cash. As he handed over the receipt, Jaden said, "Watch out for her, okay? She looks sweet, but she'll kill you."

I glared at him. *Thanks.*

Jaden winked. "Oh! And whatever you do, don't mention the word 'Twilight' to her. She may start thinking you're a werewolf or something."

That did it! If I'd been closer to him, I'd have given his armpit hair another strong tug. *The moron.*

At least Tony was polite enough not to comment until we were out the door and way out of earshot.

SEVENTEEN

♥

IT'S IN HIS KISS

We'd decided to sit on a bench not far from Old Navy to wait for Nora. I had just lathered myself in antibiotic sanitizer, hopefully killing off Jaden's germs, when Tony came back with some pretzels and asked, "So, have you really known Jaden just a few weeks?"

"A few weeks too many," I grumbled as I pulled off a piece of the warm pretzel and popped it in my mouth.

Tony chewed a bit more. "So, what'd he mean by that werewolf comment?"

"Uh . . ." *Great. Now what am I going to say?*

He smiled and took another bite. "No, wait. Don't tell me." He chewed and swallowed. "You thought he looked like a werewolf?"

Looked like one? Yeah, right. Try acted *like one!* "Something like that." I quickly bit into my pretzel so I wouldn't have to elaborate.

"Hmm . . ." Tony chuckled around another bite. "That's funny."

"What?"

"Oh." He glanced over at me and then shrugged. "I don't know. I've just always thought werewolves were kind of cool."

I almost dropped my pretzel. "Are you kidding me? You think they're cool?" *What in the world? Vampires and werewolves hate each other, don't they?*

"Yeah." He grinned. "You know, roaming around, getting a chance to run at super-fast speeds, being free and seeing the world."

"Viciously killing things by instinct—without thought—just because you're mad?" I replied with a smile. "I can see the potential there, oh yeah. What guy wouldn't love being a werewolf? Gee, as a girl, I find myself attracted to you already." I shook my head, thinking he was crazy. "That could be a pick-up line, you know? I wonder how many dates you could get, telling girls you wish you were a werewolf." I rolled my eyes and pulled off another chunk of pretzel.

Tony laughed and nudged me with his elbow. "Come on—you don't think it'd work? I bet I could get someone to go out with me."

"Yeah, right." I chuckled and tossed the piece into my mouth. "'Hey, wanna kiss? I have doggy breath.'"

Tony laughed.

"Like I said, that's just tempting me already. Hot dang!" I laughed too.

"Okay! I get it!" Tony continued to chuckle. "Werewolf is out. I don't want to know where you found out werewolves have dog breath, but believe me, I'm starting to feel real sorry for Jaden right now."

It was my turn to nudge him. "Whatever. His kisses were fine."

"Grr . . . Let's change the subject. So, what is the ultimate superhero character, then?" Tony asked as he raised his eyebrows, daring me to answer. "Or, wait! What do you see me as?"

Uh—dang! How did this happen? All at once, I wanted to be as far away from him as I could get. I quickly took another bite and hedged. "Um . . . that's hard." Chew. Chew. Chew. "The perfect hero?" *Vampire!* Chew. *Vampire, and you know it!* Chew. Chew. "Gee—uh—"

"Come on, you've gotta see me as something." He turned on the bench so we could face each other. His light brown eyes sparkled with copper flecks.

He is one hot vampire! I silently gasped and swallowed.

"How 'bout I help you?" His eyes playfully traced my features. "Do you think I have laser vision, like Cyclops? Or quick comebacks and super card-throwing action, like Gambit?"

Tony was grinning like mad, and I was having a really hard time focusing.

"Uh—an X-Men fan. Okay." *Seriously, is there a hotter guy in the world?*

"Focus." He chuckled and raised his eyebrows.

Dang! He heard me, didn't he? "Ahem. Well, I don't see you as either, actually."

"What? You're kidding! Those two are the best." He scooted closer. "Okay, tell me it's Superman, then. I could handle that."

"Superman?" I scrunched my nose.

"Ah, come on! You don't like Superman, either?"

"No! I love Superman! Really. I even like the X-Men. I was picturing you as someone else, that's all."

"Who?"

I looked down and fiddled with what was left of my pretzel. “I don’t want to say.”

Tony gently reached under my chin and brought it up. His eyes darkened, and for about ten seconds his gaze locked with mine—it was so intense I could hardly breathe. “Is he a good guy?” he finally asked.

I nodded slightly. I couldn’t speak if I wanted to.

“Is he somewhat good-looking?”

Edward? Um, yes! And then it hit me. *How cute is Tony? He wants to know if I think he’s hot.* I licked my lips and found my voice. “Oh yeah.” I really nodded that time. “He’s seriously hot.”

Tony’s eyes flew to my mouth. “Thanks,” he all but whispered. “You’re pretty hot yourself.”

Really? Warm, delicious fuzzies exploded inside me. Never had any guy been as wonderful as Tony. Never.

“Claire?”

“Yeah?”

“Let’s go.”

“Where?”

“You’ll see.”

“What about Nora?”

“Just a sec.” Tony jumped off the bench and stopped a guy and girl who were holding hands about ten feet from us. He was talking so quietly, I couldn’t understand what he was saying.

What’s he doing? Nervous, excited butterflies took the place of the warm fuzzies.

Within seconds he was standing in front of me again. “Okay, there is one. Let’s go.”

“One what? Seriously, are we just gonna leave Nora?”

He had my purse and his bag already in his hand. “We’re not leaving the mall. There’s just someplace I want to take you.

Nora'll call me when she wants to find me. Honest, we always shop like this." He held his hand out. "Now, come on. Hurry."

Smiling, I slipped my hand into his and allowed him to pull me up. "Well, lead the way then."

And he did—right to one of those cool little photo booths.

"Ta-da! Here we are."

"No way. We're going in there? Really?" I giggled. It was just too cute. "This was the surprise?"

"Yep." He sounded awfully proud of himself.

I entered the small booth and scooted over, waiting for Tony to put in the money and start the machine. I'd never realized just how small these booths were until Tony came in and sat next to me.

"The first set is just for practice, okay?"

"Okay."

I smiled for the first photo. Tony slipped his arm around my back, and I leaned in toward his chest for the second one. By the third one I was grinning at him, because he had said something stupid to make me laugh—I don't even remember what. It didn't matter, because by the fourth flash, the look he gave me could've melted ice. Neither one of us was smiling in that one. We had both stopped and stared at each other. I knew anyone could tell by the pictures that something serious was happening between Tony and me—something I don't think either of us could've predicted, had we tried.

"Wow," was all he said when he saw that last picture.

I knew it was coming. I was still humming from the powerful vibe he and I had created together. You could feel it—it was that strong. But even then, with the photo staring me in the face, I wasn't prepared for the seriousness of how attracted I was to him. It was so obvious, anyone could see it. I knew Tony could. *And that's an embarrassing thought. Mortifying, actually.*

"Do you mind if I keep this?" he asked.

"I—uh—" *Is that a good thing? Or does he want to take it home and burn it?* I didn't think I could bear having that picture burned. I was going to need something to look at when I headed back to Farmington.

"I'll let you have the next set, I promise." His smile was sweet, and he looked so genuinely happy with the thought of keeping the photo, I couldn't tell him no.

"Okay." I grinned up at him.

"Are you ready for the next set?"

"Sure." I turned around and stepped back into the booth, willing my hands not to shake with nervousness as Tony put the money in. *I can do this. I'm just going to smile and look natural and enjoy myself. This set is for me, anyway. I'm going to want proof to show my friends that I actually knew this guy.* I took a deep breath just as Tony climbed in the booth, smiling.

I watched him nervously, not sure if he was going to put his hand behind my back again or not.

He didn't. Instead he caught my gaze and sat down facing me. His smile fell. We were so close, our knees were forced outwards, and they were still touching. I knew I should turn and smile for the perfect picture, but I couldn't look away. I didn't *want* to look away.

I blinked as the first flash went off. When I opened my eyes, Tony was still staring at me. By the time the second flash came, he asked me, "Can I kiss you?"

Yes. Please. "Only if you want to."

The third flash caught his lips hovering just above mine. My eyes were closed, but he was still watching me. The fourth flash exploded just as his lips captured mine.

My heart soared. *Tony Russo is kissing me!* I couldn't believe it.

When we broke apart, he grinned widely, and I rubbed my lips together, enjoying the tingling sensation. One thing was very certain—no matter what I had thought earlier, Tony Russo was not a vampire. His lips were too warm and soft.

All at once I felt crazy cool, like the most beautiful girl in the world. My heart was racing, and my cheeks were red—I could feel them, but I didn't care. Tony Russo had just kissed me. *Me!* Out of all the girls he could have chosen, he chose me.

He shook his head a bit and then looked around, as though he'd forgotten we were in a photo booth. When he caught my eyes again, he grinned a devastatingly hot grin. "Now those pictures, I've gotta see." He grabbed the strip of photos as soon as they came out of the machine.

His arm was around my back and clasping my shoulder as we both chuckled at our faces in the moments before the kiss. I grew all warm and fuzzy again when I saw the way Tony's eyes watched my closed ones. There was something meaningful about that look—I couldn't quite put my finger on it, but it was something especially wonderful.

"Wanna trade?" he whispered in my ear as he brought out the other strip of pictures.

"No way." I chuckled, grateful for the pictures I had. You could only see half of Tony, but it was such a special moment, it made up for not being able to really show him off.

"What are we going to do?" he quietly asked as he slipped his hand from my shoulder to my arm.

I knew what he meant—he didn't have to explain himself. We hardly knew each other, and I lived a gazillion miles away. Not the best start to a relationship.

"I don't know." Unbelievable sadness washed over me.

Tony muttered something under his breath and pulled

me into him. I relaxed into his warm, strong hug. “Whatever happens,” he murmured into my hair, “I’ll never forget you. I couldn’t, even if I tried.”

“Well, I know one thing we can do,” I said as I snuggled closer to him.

“What’s that?”

“Get to know each other.” My hands drew lazy circles on his back. “You know, our likes and dislikes.”

“Good idea.” He straightened up a bit. “You ask the first question, and then we’ll both answer it.”

“Oh, um . . . I don’t know.” I pulled back a little to look up at him and then asked the first question that popped in my mind. “What’s your favorite color?”

“Easy. Orange.”

“Orange?” That surprised me. “Really?”

“Yeah, I like it. It’s bold and friendly at the same time.” Tony stepped back and held my hand, then slowly guided me over to a bench against the wall. “So, what’s yours?”

“Silver.”

“Silver? Cool. That’s different.”

“You were expecting me to say pink, weren’t you?” I laughed.

“I didn’t know what to expect. But I like silver.” He cleared his throat. “Okay, my turn. What’s your favorite movie?”

“Twilight.”

He smiled and nodded. “Hence the werewolf fascination.”

“Eew!” I bumped him with my shoulder. He retaliated by bringing his arm around me and pulling me up against his side. “For your information,” I informed him, “I happen to like the vampire. As a matter of fact, I think he’s the perfect super—” *Oh my gosh! What am I saying? He’ll freak if he realizes I thought he was a vampire!*

"What? Wait a minute. You don't like werewolves, but you like vampires? Isn't that a little contradictory?"

I sat up. "What do you mean? Werewolves and vampires are like night and day."

"Well, not when it comes to their food choices. Both prefer blood." He shuddered. "Vampires sort of creep me out—they're so cold and lifeless. At least a werewolf has a body and a heart." He turned slightly to look at me better. "You really like vampires?" He said it like he thought it was a disease.

"Well, I'm not in a coven or anything, but yeah, I like them." He was seriously stomping all over a touchy subject. "So, what's *your* favorite movie?" I asked, deciding to change the topic and get back to where we were.

"I like *Pirates of the Caribbean.* All of them."

I nodded my head in agreement. It was my turn again. "Um, okay . . . what's your favorite food?"

"Bagel sandwiches."

"Okay, those are good," I said. "I prefer nachos—with jalapeños."

"Favorite hobby? Mine's volunteering at the Y. You are coming to the game, right?"

"You mean tomorrow?" I smiled. "Yeah, I'll be there."

"Cool. So, you?"

"Hmm . . . I have a lot of hobbies, actually, but I think my favorite would be cooking."

"Cooking? No way." He chuckled. "I've totally kissed the cook. So, what's your favorite thing to cook?"

I laughed. "Nachos."

"Oh, duh. Okay, your turn."

"What's your favorite type of music?"

Tony shrugged. "Anything. Everything."

I rolled my eyes. "Come on, give me a band, a group, a

song—something."

"Nickelback. Do you know them?"

"Nickelback? Uh, yeah! They're awesome. Anyone else?"

"Sure. The Beatles, Sting, Madonna, Elvis, Lifehouse, Bruno Mars, Black Eyed Peas, Chris Daughtry—I don't know. It just depends on the song and my mood." He shrugged again. "You?"

"I noticed you didn't mention any country stars. You do realize I'm from New Mexico, right? It's practically all we listen to down there. So I have to say, like, Lady Antebellum, Carrie Underwood, Taylor Swift, Rascal Flatts—you know, all of them."

"You don't like any rock or pop music, then?" Tony asked, looking uncomfortable.

Great. He probably hates country. "Sure, um . . . Lifehouse and Nickelback, too. I like Christina Perri, and anything Selena Gomez sings. Oh! My sister Cass had this new single on her iPod, like a month ago, from this brand-new band, and it was really good. You have to listen to it. I wonder if she brought her iPod with her? I bet she did. When we get back, remind me to have you listen to it. She was telling me the lead singer wrote all the songs, and he's starting to get national attention for it."

"Really?" Tony seemed interested. "What's his name?"

"What *is* his name . . . I can't remember. But I think I remember the name of the band—it was something mean-sounding. Like, like North—Northfighting something." *I'm such a dork. Why can't I remember the name?*

"Um, do you mean Northanger Alibi?"

EIGHTEEN
♥
TOTAL ECLIPSE OF THE HEART

"Yes! You know them? You've heard their music? Isn't it good?" I gushed.

Tony looked like I had just slapped him. I had never seen anyone so stunned before.

"What's wrong?"

"We have to go." He stood up.

"What?"

"I just noticed the time—I was supposed to be back ten minutes ago." He pulled out his phone and started dialing. "Let's get Nora, and then we'll head out."

By the time Nora joined us, she was pretty ticked. "Tony, if I'd have known you were only going to be able to stay an hour or two, we'd have driven ourselves here."

"Look, I'm sorry. I didn't think we'd be here that long."

She stared at him as if his head was on backwards. "Are you kidding? This is a mall, Tony. A *mall.* Of course we're going to be here a while. You know tha—" She stopped mid-sentence and glanced at me. "What? What happened?" she asked.

"Happened?" I wasn't aware I was making a face or anything. "What do you mean?"

Her eyes narrowed in on Tony. "Something has happened. Spill." She pointed her finger at her brother. "There's no way you didn't know we would be a while—that's just an excuse, a very stupid excuse to get away from here. What's going on?"

Nora wasn't the only one ticked. "Drop it, okay? Nothing has happened, or is happening." He ran his hands through his hair and flicked a glance at me. That quick look spoke volumes.

Oh my gosh! He does want away from me. Why?

"Dang it! You kissed her, didn't you?" She surprised us both by throwing that at him. "You kissed her, and now you're regretting it."

"Nora!" The glare he sent her could've sizzled paint. "Shut up. Okay?"

I'd heard enough.

Tony was furious—*too* furious. Something was wrong, like she'd hit a nerve or something. Maybe he *was* regretting kissing me. One thing was for certain—I wasn't going to stand around and listen to them battle it out. I grabbed my purse and spun on my heel. They didn't even see me leave.

"Why should I shut up?!" Nora was practically shouting. "You're the idiot who went and kissed someone you hardly knew—someone who needs to know a few things about you before you basically commit yourself!"

"What's the big deal? It was just a kiss. I'm not going out with her or anything, so just lighten up."

Just a kiss? I walked faster. I really didn't want to hear any more.

"You know, Tony, if it was any other guy, I'd believe that. But since it's you—and knowing your history with kissing—

don't you think you should get off it a bit and come down and talk to the girl? You know, share things, instead of running from them—"

I turned the corner and was thankfully saved—the dull roar of the mall was the only sound I could hear. I didn't usually run from things, either, but there was just something about this mall that made me really grateful to escape. And if there was ever a girl who needed to escape, it was me.

"Whoa, Claire! Where's the fire?"

I was surprised to see Jaden bounding up to me. "What are you doing?" I asked.

"I'm heading home. Boss let me go a little early. What are *you* doing? Where's your boyfriend?"

"He's not my boyfriend." I walked faster, and Jaden kept step with me.

"Did you guys have a fight or something?"

"No."

"Yeah, well, you look mad."

"I'm not mad, okay?" *More like livid, furious, hurt, upset . . .*

"Then why are you running away?"

Does he have to be such a dork?

"I don't know, okay? I'm just leaving, that's all." My phone rang. It was Tony. *Dang.* I ignored it. "Jaden, could you do me a favor and drive me home, please?"

He stopped, causing me to turn around and stop, too.

Don't make me beg. I just want out of here.

He folded his arms over his chest. My phone kept ringing. "Are you saying you trust me to drive?" he asked skeptically.

No. But it's far superior to listening to those two fight. "Yes. As long as you follow the speed limit."

"Hmm . . . that'll be hard. But I promise to try."

That's better than nothing. "Okay, and I promise not to

maim you as long as you don't try to get us killed."

Jaden laughed. "Done. Let's go." He waved his hand at the entrance. "My car's parked out here."

"Thanks." I followed him through the doors. My phone stopped ringing, only to start up again.

"Are you going to answer that?" he asked over his shoulder.

I shrugged. "I don't know. Probably not."

"Is he worried?"

"Maybe."

"Do you care?"

"Stop it. Okay? I really don't want to talk about Tony right now—can we talk about something else, please?"

"Sure," he said. "Do I get a kiss when this is all over?"

Ugh. I rolled my eyes. "On second thought, let's talk about Tony."

"Good." Jaden sounded smug, like he was hoping I'd say that. "So, how come I know that guy? Why does he seem so familiar?"

Never mind. I don't want to talk about him. "Um, I don't know. You're not the only one to recognize him, though—he seems familiar to a lot of people. But before you ask, no, I don't know who he is. He won't tell me."

"Ah! So that's why you're running."

I could see Jaden's car up ahead. "No. That's not why." *Okay, maybe a little.* "I'm running because . . ." *I'm running because I think I like Tony a whole lot more than he likes me. And that hurts.*

"Yeah? You were saying?"

We reached the car, and Jaden unlocked it. In silence, I climbed in. My phone had stopped ringing. As soon as he shut the door, I sent Tony a text.

dnt wry bout me. got a ride. headn
home now.

I turned off my phone so I wouldn't have to read anything he sent right away.

"You're running because . . . ?" Jaden was nothing if not persistent.

"Because I'd rather not talk about it right now."

"Oh, so we're back to that again, are we?" He threw me an arch look as he started the car and put it in gear. "So, uh, when exactly do I get that kiss?"

"You're kidding me, right?" I crossed one leg over the other and turned to face him. "If I don't talk, you're gonna keep harassing me into giving you a kiss—until eventually you'll steal one anyway?"

Jaden smiled as he looked behind him and backed out of the parking space. "That wasn't exactly my fantasy, but I'm not stupid—we'll adapt to yours."

He's such a dork. "Ha ha. Very funny."

"Don't worry. If you think I'm just teasing you, I'll prove it. I have never been more serious in my entire life. I'd kiss you right now if I wasn't driving."

"And I will seriously kick your butt again if you try anything, Jaden." I flipped my hair and looked out the window. "Believe me, that was just rule number one. There are at least thirty-five more that I know of, and they're all just as painful as the last one."

"So basically it's all down to if I like living dangerously or not?"

I could hear the grin in his voice. I decided not to answer him—it was only egging him on more anyway. Instead, I focused on the passing scenery as we pulled out of the mall parking lot.

After a few moments of silence, he tried another tactic. "Well, what did your boyfriend say to my werewolf comment?"

I willed myself not to roll my eyes again. Instead, I took a deep breath. "Nothing, actually. It turns out he thinks werewolves are cool. He actually liked the idea of being one."

Jaden started laughing. "I bet that got you in a huff. I can't imagine you thinking he was anything like me."

"No way. Just the opposite, actually," I muttered as I traced the window ledge with my finger.

"Well, that explains a lot."

I turned in time to watch Jaden shake his head in disbelief. "What does?" I couldn't help asking.

He was still shaking his head. "Why didn't I think of it before? Of course you would've thought it. I mean, that's why he gets the girl, right?" Jaden actually looked happy, like he'd discovered some secret.

"What the heck are you talking about? Your brain jumps around too fast for me to follow."

"How old are you?" he surprised me by asking.

"Sixteen. Why?"

He nodded. "See, this is what I'm talking about. This is why you don't lose your heart to somebody younger than you are, right here." He pointed at me, as if he were talking to a whole crowd of people.

"You are so weird, you know that?" I answered defensively.

He really laughed then, like, threw his head back and laughed. "I'm weird? Me? Look who's talking, princess." He glanced at the road and then over at me. "You're living in a book. Anything you have ever imagined or experienced is all in a book. A fictional story."

"Whatever. That's just—"

"So, does he know you think he's a vampire?"

My jaw dropped. "W–what?" My voice came out in a squeak. "Does who know what?"

Jaden smirked and shook his head. "Don't try to act all innocent. You and I both know you think Tony's a vampire."

Not anymore. "No, I don't!" I protested. "Not at all. There's no way. His lips are—" I stopped on a gasp.

"Ah, another light goes on. That's why you're not into my kisses anymore. Bella has kissed her Edward."

I huffed. "You think you're so funny, don't you? Really, I think you should consider becoming a comedian. You've got talent."

"Flattery gets you everywhere, baby." His smug smile made my fingers itch to slap him.

Violence is not the answer. Violence is not the answer. I took another couple of deep breaths. It didn't work. I still wanted to kill him.

"So, that leaves me as the best friend, doesn't it?" Jaden shrugged as if this were all some joke. "That's not a bad place to be, I guess." He looked over at me, beaming stupidly. "You look a little uptight there, Bella. Oops. I mean, Claire. Want me to show you how to ride a motorcycle? Or wait! What else did he do? Oh yeah—I know some cliffs you can dive off. Of course, I'm not sure how deep they go—like, I'm not going to do it. There may be rocks and stuff at the bottom, but since you're so depressed about Ed—er, *Tony* right now, I'll be happy to take you there."

He acted as though he was going to change lanes.

I wasn't sure this was a better trade-off. *The more I think about it, I should've taken the ride home with Tony and Nora. So what if they yelled at each other the whole way and acted like I wasn't there. At least it was better than the alternative. Lucky me—now I've got a werewolf wannabe who is enjoying every moment of torturing me. Ugh!* The worst part was, he had the upper hand, and he knew it.

"I'm not depressed," I mumbled.

"What was that?"

"I said, I'm not depressed." I was louder this time. Much louder. I almost yelled it. "I haven't known the guy long enough to be depressed."

"Really? Then why are you sulking?"

"I'm not sulking, either! For crying out loud, will you just let up, please?" I put my head in my hands and leaned forward—or as far as the seatbelt would let me. It wasn't the exact dramatic, dejected pose I was going for, but it was good enough.

"All right." Jaden took a deep breath. "I'm sorry. I'll leave you alone." He muttered something under his breath and then said, "I shouldn't even be speaking to you after your stunt in Old Navy, but I can't help myself." He waited a few more seconds for me to say something. When I didn't, he asked, "You want to talk about it?"

"I don't know."

"Come on," Jaden coaxed. "I'm your best friend, remember?"

I snorted. *Yeah, right.*

"So, imagine that I am. What would you have said to your best friend at home? I know you're dying to talk to somebody right now, so spit it out. We have a twenty-minute drive, anyway. You don't want to go the whole way in silence, do you?"

Fine. I sighed and sat up, rubbing my hands on my legs. "You are like the pushiest person on the planet—you know that, right?"

He chuckled. "So, talk already."

NINETEEN ♥ TRUSTING A WOLF

"Grr . . ." I took a deep breath and blew it out. "It's not what you think. Tony doesn't like me like you think he does."

"Oh, no. Guys definitely don't kiss girls we like. Nope. We only kiss the ones who bug us."

"I wish." Then, for no reason, I giggled. "No, okay, so he likes me—but I don't think he wants to."

"Okay, now that I understand."

"Hey!" I shoved Jaden playfully in the arm. "You know you love me."

"Hmm . . . no comment." He grinned and looked back at the road. "So, what makes you think he doesn't like you?"

"I don't know. This whole him-being-somebody-famous thing—at least, I think he's somebody famous—has really thrown me off. I mean, it was okay when he was just this vampire guy, which I know he's not now."

Jaden was wise enough not to say anything. He just shook his head.

"But he's really serious about not telling anyone who he is. He said he'd break his contract if he does. But Nora says—"

"That's his sister, right?" Jaden interrupted. "The chick who came in and was hitting on Joe?"

"She was?" I smiled. *Good for her!* "Um, yes. That's his twin sister."

"Ah, okay. So he'll break his contract if he tells anyone?"

"Yeah, except Nora says he won't, and that he should tell me. Then, get this—she knows like everything that happens to him, like *everything*. It's why I was positive he was a vampire, because it's like they can read minds. So, there we were after the photo booth—"

"Whoa, Bessie. Slow down. There *who* was after the photo booth? And what photo booth are you talking about?"

"The one where Tony kissed me. Here." I leaned down and pulled the strip of pictures out of my purse. "See? Our first kiss." I waved it under his nose.

Jaden grabbed the long, skinny sheet of photos and set them on the steering wheel. He glanced down a few times until he had seen them all. "Wow." He handed the pictures back to me. "I've got to hand it to him. That's a pretty cool place for a first kiss. You've even got proof." He cleared his throat and looked straight ahead.

All at once I felt like a huge idiot. "I'm sorry." I quickly slipped the photos back in my purse.

"For what?" Jaden shrugged. "I'm your best friend, remember? You're supposed to show me stuff like you kissing another guy."

"Oh yeah." I looked down and fiddled with the strap of the seatbelt.

"Okay, so what happened next? After Nora came?"

"Oh." I brought my head up. "So, Tony and I hug a bit

because we're kind of freaked out over the photos and how cool they were—anyway, so then we decided it was time to get to know each other. And as we were asking each other a bunch of different questions, Tony just jumps up and freaks out, saying he has to go and that he's late for something. Which, okay, so we've all been late before—it was just weird, you know?"

"So then Nora came?"

"Yeah. Well, Tony calls her and she comes to where we are, and she gets seriously mad. Like yelling and everything. And I'm standing there wishing I wasn't standing there—because it's way stupid when those two go at it."

"Well, they're brother and sister. Aren't they supposed—"

"Not in front of me," I interrupted. "It's stupid."

"All right." Jaden lifted his hands off the wheel for a second. "It's stupid. Then what happened?"

"Then Nora starts accusing Tony of lying and trying to leave early, and she wants to know what happened to make him want to leave. Anyway, she figures out we've kissed each other, and that makes her really mad, because he's had virgin lips this whole time, and—"

"Wait! No way! Mr. Vampire has virgin lips?" Jaden looked like he was going to burst with glee. I could tell he thought it was hilarious.

"Not anymore," I pointed out.

"You hussy."

"Whatever." I rolled my eyes. "Anyway—"

"Anyway. Go on, I'm listening." He smiled innocently at me. If I had a brick, I'd have thrown it at that smile.

"So Nora's mad because—"

"—Cold Lips has kissed you—"

"Hot Lips, okay? His lips were very warm."

"Ah, again. Another lightbulb flickers to life." He nodded.

"Now you know he's really human."

"You know you're really an annoying best friend, don't you?"

"I try my best. Now hurry up—I'm listening."

"So, Nora's mad because he kissed me—mainly because she doesn't think we've known each other long enough for that kind of commitment, at least on his part."

"So she doesn't think her brother should kiss you because you live so far away—that he'd just be wasting his kisses on you?"

"Maybe that's what she was getting at. I don't know. All I do know is, she was mad. And they started fighting. So I walked away."

"What'd they do?"

"They kept arguing. They didn't even know I'd left. Of course, that's when I heard Tony freak out and yell that it didn't matter anyway, because he wasn't going out with me and it was only a kiss." I heaved a sigh. *Okay, so that hurt. Right there. The one thing that bothered me most.*

"So that's why you didn't answer your phone?"

"Yeah, well, I didn't need to hear *that* again."

"But don't you think he's trying to call you now?"

I looked down at my purse. Two big, stupid tears started to form in my eyes. *Don't cry! Don't cry!* "Probably."

"Are you going to let him apologize?"

I blinked, and one of the tears fell. I quickly turned my head to look out the window. I allowed the little guy to follow a path down my cheek. I wasn't about to wipe it in front of Jaden.

"Look, Claire." Jaden took a deep breath. "This goes against the grain, saying this, but chances are, he just said that to get Nora off his back. And chances are, this guy really, really likes you—and has probably fallen for you. Hard."

The other tear fell. "That's impossible." I tried to make my voice sound normal. "We haven't known each other long enough. Nora's right. He can't fall for me." Two more big tears filled up my eyes again.

"Really?" Jaden's voice was gentle. "It sounds like you're trying to convince yourself." He paused a moment and then asked, "Claire, have you fallen for him?"

Yes! I closed my eyes. Now tears streamed down my cheeks. "No, I couldn't have. I don't even know who is he, do I?" I gave up. I didn't care if Jaden could see or not. I sniffed and wiped the tears off my face. *Who are you, Tony Russo? And why won't you tell me? What are you afraid of, anyway?*

{♥}

By the time I got home, I was in no mood to talk to anyone. In fact, my bed seemed like the perfect place to crash. Jaden didn't even try to walk me to the door, thank goodness. He just made some comment about texting me later to see if I was okay. With a huge sigh, I entered the cottage and walked right past Cassidy, who was reading on the couch. *Good. That means I'll have the room all to myself.*

"You're home early," she called after me.

I headed straight for the stairs. "Yep."

"Any reason?"

"Not feeling good," I answered. "I'm gonna lie down for a bit."

"Okay. I'm gonna stay here and read."

Perfect. I marched up the stairs and plopped face down on the bed. My purse smacked the pillow next to me. *Ugh. My phone. Should I turn it on?* I pulled it out of the purse and turned it over in my hand. *What if Tony has the most amazing excuse ever? What if he's begging my forgiveness and flat out tells me I'm the most beautifulest, wonderfulest, kindest person he's ever known, and he can't stop thinking about me?* I smiled. *That would be seriously cool.* My smile fell. *What if it isn't excuses and apologies and flatteries? What if he is just worried about getting me home so Roger and Darlene won't be mad?* I threw the phone onto Cassidy's bed without turning it on. *Never mind.* In some ways, not knowing what he said was better than facing the truth.

In disgust, I heaved myself off the bed and pattered into the luxurious bathroom. My eyes were drawn instantly to the large bathtub. That's what I needed. I collected my things and the third book in the Twilight series; Cassidy had just started the fourth. I headed back into the bathroom, turned on the faucet, and poured some bubble bath into the tub. Immediately, thousands of sparkling little bubbles burst to life. I let out an exhausted sigh.

In no time at all, I was sinking happily into the bath, *Eclipse* in my hand, ready to escape the world around me. I mean, nothing was better than fiction, right?

About an hour later I wandered out of the bathroom—dressed, with bare feet, and a tie pulling my hair up in a messy bun. My phone was still on Cassidy's bed. This time curiosity overrode common sense. I had to know what Tony had been trying to say. Maybe it was the hour of reading and seeing the struggle in Edward that did it—I don't know. But all at once I wanted to know what my vampire—*okay, human, but can't I still have a bit of fantasy left?*—wrote to me. I scooped up the phone and plunked down on my bed, crossing my feet beneath me.

I took a deep breath. *Okay, so here's the deal. I'm not going to get upset either way. If he likes me and has showered me with millions of compliments, I'm going to smile and remain calm. If he's just concerned about my safety and worried he'll get in trouble, then I'm going to smile and remain calm for that, too. Got it?* I took another breath and closed my eyes. Blindly, I pushed the button and heard the phone chime to life in my hand. I waited.

For five minutes I waited with my eyes closed to hear the chimes announcing Tony's text messages arriving in my mailbox. None came. *Huh?* Warily, I opened one eye and scanned the messages I had already received. There were no new messages from Tony. Scanning through my voicemail, I realized he didn't leave a message there, either.

What in the world? He didn't send me a message at all? Not at all? Not even an "Are you okay?" text? Holy cow! He has no idea who I went home with—how does he know I'm even safe?

And then it hit me full force, like a ton of bricks. Tony didn't care about me. I had the evidence right in my hand. Here I'd thought he'd be worrying himself sick. Nope. In fact, after reviewing the evidence, it would seem he was relieved.

Dejected, I tossed the phone across the room. It landed with a thud on the overstuffed chair. After I'd seen that it landed safely, I dramatically threw myself backward onto the bed in despair. *Why did I ever turn my phone on?* It was so much better to not know what he thought. *Okay, I have been the biggest dork in the history of dorks.*

My eyes stubbornly filled with tears again, and I closed them, not ready to deal with such an emotional disappointment. Discouraged beyond belief—for a girl who'd just promised herself moments before that she'd smile and remain calm no matter what happened—I turned on my side and curled around a thick pillow, hoping my silent tears wouldn't stain the smooth satin surface.

When I first awoke about forty minutes later, I thought the radio was on. My eyes blinked open, and I listened to the sound—it was far away, almost as though it was in another room. I groaned and pulled my watch off the bedside table to see how long I had slept. *Good grief, it was way past time to get up.* When I sat up, the music seemed to get louder. It was oddly familiar, like I had heard the song before, just not the version that was playing now.

The room was still empty. I could tell Cassidy hadn't been up to check on me. *Good.* I slipped off the bed to wash my face. As I walked closer to the window, the music got louder. *What's going on? Is someone having a party outside?* I moved the curtains and peered out the window.

Oh my gosh! Is he for real?

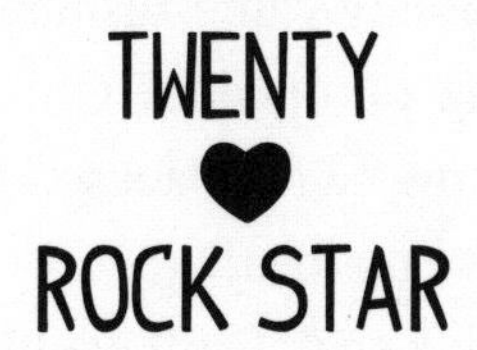

TWENTY ♥ ROCK STAR

I quickly threw open the window, engulfing myself in the glorious music below. Tony grinned up at me, jamming on a guitar, and continued to sing the song I had been raving about earlier from the new band, Northanger Alibi.

I didn't have a heart until I met you.
That smile is killin' me too.
I can't look away.
Can I always stay?
I can't look away.
I need to stay.
I didn't have a heart until I met you.
Come on, girl, I need you.

I smiled. *He's good! He's really good. Like, almost as good as the band's lead singer.*

With a flash, I remembered the singer's name—Jackson

Russolini. My smiled faltered. Why that name caused me to stop and stare hard at Tony, I don't know. But it did. *Oh my gosh! Is he—? He can't be! I mean, there's no way he's Jackson from—*

"Hey, Claire!" Cassidy came rushing in the room. "Have you seen what's going on outside? Oh! You're looking now. Holy cow! Did you know he was Jackson Russolini? I'm totally freaking out—you have no idea!"

"Is he? Do you think so?" I still couldn't believe it.

"Uh, duh!" She joined me at the window and groaned. "Look how hot he is playing that guitar!" She turned and grabbed me by the shoulders. "Claire! We totally know someone famous!" She clutched tighter and began to jump up and down. "I can't believe it! I'm gonna freak, seriously! I'm gonna die right now! Eeeh!"

I hardly paid any attention to her. My sole focus was on the amazing look Tony was giving me from below. It had to have been the most magnificent grin in the whole world.

The key changed in the music, and I knew he was gearing up for the guitar solo. As fast as I could, I shook my sister's hands off and dashed down the stairs and out the front door. There was nothing I loved more than an awesome guitar solo, no matter what music genre.

Tony smiled as he approached me, his head bobbing with the beat. I liked the way he bit his bottom lip and scrunched up his nose when he got to the really complicated part. *He loves this! He's such a natural, too.* I could tell he'd been playing for a long time.

"Wahoo!" I hollered and clapped, which made him smile more. It blew me away to see him like this—so in his element and so talented. I'd never seen anyone as hot as Tony Russo was right then.

When he got to the chorus again, I laughed and sang along. He took another step toward me, strumming and jammin'. We were only about two feet apart when he did a quick break in the melody and sang the chorus again, this time straight at me, like he wanted me to really hear what he was saying. I listened while the spark in his eyes subconsciously pulled me closer.

I didn't have a heart until I met you.
That smile is killin' me too.
I can't look away.
Can I always stay?
I can't look away.
I need to stay.
I didn't have a heart until I met you.
Come on, girl, I need you.

He finished with an extra jolt and a strum that he playfully held out as his voice matched the note on the word "you." After yanking his guitar up, he did a half bow, his eyes still holding mine. For a split second, the world around us was frozen and silent. No one else existed except Tony and me. *I can't believe he sang to me! Oh my gosh!* A splattering of applause erupted all around us, breaking the hold he had on me.

As I looked around, I was surprised to see a group of neighborhood children clapping on the lawn. An older couple with their dog was also applauding by the driveway, but my own family and friends were cheering the loudest.

"Tony! Way to go," Roger hollered from behind me.

I didn't even know he was home. I stepped aside and watched as he rushed past to clap Tony on the shoulder.

Darlene was all eager smiles and glee. "That was the best thing we've heard in a long time!" she exclaimed as she ran past me to give him a hug.

Tony shyly took it all in stride, especially when Cassidy ran over, jumping up and down and acting like a complete teenage crush. The more praise he got, the more the neighbors warmed up as well. Soon everyone was around him and cheering for him and asking for his autograph. Only I stood back. He noticed, too. Every chance he got, he looked up at me and then smiled. It was cute to see that he was still thinking of me.

After a few minutes, I did notice a problem starting. He was beginning to attract even more attention from passing neighbors and people spreading the news. Just when I was beginning to think I'd never get a chance to talk to him, a man approached with his camera phone.

Apparently that was Tony's limit. He backed off, and after handing his guitar to Roger, he moved toward the porch near me, thanking everyone graciously with a little wave. People everywhere broke out into applause again. Tony smiled, grabbed my hand, and maneuvered us into the house. I had a quick glimpse of Roger and Darlene bathed in glowing admiration from the natives as Tony shut the door.

"Sorry about that." He looked worried. "I wasn't expecting so many people to be around."

"Well, you did come here in broad daylight," I pointed out.

"Yeah, but . . ." He shook his head. "I kind of pictured that differently. You know, I thought I'd get you all to myself."

I laughed. "I'm here now."

"Yeah, I know." He grinned and then walked past to poke his head around the curtains.

"What's wrong?" I asked as he came back, looking dejected.

"Plan B isn't going to work now."

"Plan B?"

"Yeah, I—" He sheepishly looked down. "I kind of had a couple of plans for tonight."

"Really?"

He peeked up at me. "Plan A was to get you to talk to me. If that worked, I was gonna move on to Plan B."

"What's that?"

"Well, I had planned to take you on a picnic in the park, but I'm thinking I'm not going to be able to leave anytime soon. Those kids are all around my car." He didn't sound mad, just disappointed.

Aw. My heart melted. I cleared my throat. "Well, there's a small back yard, if you want to try that."

"Really?" His eyes gleamed as he raised his head. "Yeah, that'd be cool. Where is it?" He tugged my hand and pulled me with him toward the back of the house.

"Not there!" I chuckled and stopped near the closet to put on a pair of flip-flops. "You have to go through the kitchen." I gently maneuvered him the right way. "In here."

We were out back and walking on the small stone path that led to a canopied swing before either of us spoke again. "Thanks for talking to me," Tony all but whispered.

I didn't know what to say, so I settled on, "That's okay."

As we reached the swing, he stepped aside and allowed me to sit down. I thought he would automatically join me, but instead he asked, "Do you mind if I sit with you? I know I don't deserve to, so I totally understand if you say no, it's just—"

"Yes." I scooted over. "Sit down." I patted the seat next to me for emphasis. The swing rocked and jerked a bit as he joined me.

"Um, so I need to explain a few things first." He glanced over at me and then nervously began to rock the swing.

I matched his rhythm. It was comforting to be sitting next to him, even after the day I'd had. "Okay." I was all ears.

Tony took a deep breath. "Let's start with today and that kiss."

I blushed and looked away, not sure I wanted to hear what he had to say.

"No, wait. I'm going to start before that—way before that, like two years ago, when I first vowed I wouldn't kiss a girl until, well, until . . ." His voice trailed off.

Until . . . ? Instantly, I was reminded of what Nora had said earlier about him not kissing a girl until he could—I was too embarrassed to even think it.

When he found his voice again, he was staring right at me. "Until I thought I could love her."

Oh my gosh! He actually said it!

"Well, I guess what I'm trying to say—and failing miserably—is that you're the first person I've felt that possibility with, you know?"

I was confused—baffled, actually—and I found myself wanting a straight answer. "But why me? I don't get it."

Tony must've seen I was serious because he shook his head and answered truthfully. "I don't know. Honestly, I've asked myself that a lot. Why now? And why a girl who doesn't even live here? That's the hardest part for me." He straightened up a bit and turned to face me. "I think it's just because you're you. You're steady, and like today, just now, when everyone else was around me, you stood back and waited. You're—I don't know—security for me, or something. Look, ever since this whole band thing happened—which I promise to get to in a bit—my life has changed, really changed. Everything around me was hard to control, and people were everywhere, always around and laughing and excited and, well, they wanted me because of who I was, not because of me. Do you understand what I'm saying?"

I nodded. "I think so."

"Then you came along, and you didn't even care about me, or think about me, or—or anything. And I don't know, it was nice. You were nice and spunky and funny and tough, and I just found myself drawn to you. I wanted to talk to you and be by you. And anyway, it surprised me when you told me you'd kissed that Jaden guy. It surprised me big time, because all at once I was jealous. That's when it hit me that I wanted to kiss you—and I would've then, not impulsively, either. I decided long ago that if I ever met a girl I wanted to kiss, and the opportunity presented itself, I was going to take it. I just hadn't found you, and then the opportunity wasn't really there, I guess, until today."

I knew my face was beet red. I lowered my eyes and focused on the grass. "But what about Nora? Why doesn't she want you to kiss me? Did I make her mad or something?"

"Nora? No way. She likes you. Really."

She has a funny way of showing it.

He sighed and ran his fingers through his hair. "She's just worried about me—about the band. Look, I uh—kind of risked a lot by coming here. And she knows it. She thinks it's stupid, and maybe she's right. I mean, that's why I came, because for the first time, I could see it from her point of view, and it *is* stupid."

"What, the contract you guys were talking about?"

"Yeah, that. Actually, it isn't legal or anything—it has to do with my mom and dad. Back when the band was first starting out, we were attracting the notice of a lot of people—so much so, my mom and dad freaked." Tony leaned back in the swing, and the rocking motion slowed almost to a stop. "They promised to let me do this—become a sort-of rock star—if I promised not to get a big head about it. They had seen so many celebs lose their cool and go crazy, and they were worried about me, because I was so young."

I'd be worried, too. Who could ignore the tragic stories of the different teen/young adult celebrities in the pages of gossip magazines?

"Anyway, I had to promise not to tell anyone who I was—well, that and keep my grades up." He grinned. "The thing is, when I was on stage, I could be me, but when I wasn't performing, I had to keep a real low profile. It was the only way they'd let me do it. I haven't even seen much of the money, either. It's all wrapped up in a bank account for college, or life or whatever."

"Are you kidding? Does that bother you?"

"The money?" He shrugged. "No. It's not like they're hoarding it or anything. It's my account. Their names aren't even on it. I just don't get to spend it on sports cars and stuff."

I had never heard of anything like that before. "So, what happens if you do, or if you broke this contract with them?"

"Yeah, that." He cleared his throat. "See now, that's a bit harder. They've always threatened to pull the plug on the band if I told anyone about it—"

"Wait! But you've told me, right? And all those neighbors, and—"

"Actually, I haven't told you—I've *shown* you, and I'm thinking you put the pieces together. But it won't count anyway. My mom and dad are going to be ticked. They would definitely consider singing under your window in front of everyone to be showing off." He leaned forward and rested his elbows on his knees, his head in his hands. "I'm seventeen. I'm a minor. They can very easily step in and pull me out of the band for a couple of years."

"So is your name really Jackson Russolini?"

"It's Anthony Jackson Russo—they just added the 'lini' part to make it sound cooler."

I pushed him in the arm. "So, why'd you come here? I didn't need to know! Sheesh. You're in the top ten, for crying out loud!"

"Top three, actually. I just got the text today."

"Really? You've made it to the top three? Holy cow!"

"I know." He smiled. "It's kind of crazy cool, huh?"

"Tony!" I shoved him again. "Why would you ruin your whole career to come here and see me? What about the other band members?"

"You know why?" He turned to fully face me. "Because for the first time in my life, I found something I love more than playing—and I was losing her. That's why."

TWENTY-ONE

♥

LOVE BITES

Oh my gosh! My heart stopped beating, and my breathing was replaced by short, silent gasps.

"Claire, I was an idiot today. I deserved to have you walk away—actually, I wouldn't have respected you if you'd stayed. I was the biggest, stupidest idiot that has ever existed. When I turned around and you were gone, I freaked. I totally lost it. I knew then that losing you to my stupidity would've been the biggest mistake of my life. All at once, playing the guitar or being in some band didn't matter if I couldn't have the one real thing in my life."

He grabbed my hands and held them between his. "You don't know what a heart attack you gave me when I couldn't find you and you wouldn't answer your phone. I was running up and down that mall until your text came through. And boy, did everything really sink in then. I knew I was a loser—I knew it—especially if you were willing to ride home with someone else." He pinched the bridge of his nose and closed his eyes.

"Just tell me you went home with the werewolf, okay? Tell me you didn't hitch a ride with some stranger. I couldn't bear it if I thought you'd gone off with just anyone—"

"It was Jaden. Don't worry." I grinned. *How cute is he?*

Tony heaved a big sigh of relief and opened his eyes. "I stopped in at Old Navy once the idea came into my head that you might've taken off with him, and thankfully the manager said Jaden left around the same time you did. And why'd you turn off your phone, anyway? Wait! Don't answer that—I have a more important question. Not that it matters, but I'd just like to know anyway. Did the guy try to kiss you again?"

I giggled. "What? After I'd kicked his butt earlier? He wouldn't dare."

Tony shook his head and laughed. "What did you do to that guy, anyway? I'd never seen anyone that big look so scared of a girl before."

"Nope." I grinned. "I'm not telling. A lady doesn't reveal her secrets."

Tony smiled, shaking his head in amazement. "Man, I love you." His eyes seared into mine a moment before he looked away.

Oh my gosh! Oh my gosh! Oh my gosh! I'd forgotten how to breathe again.

When he locked his eyes with mine once more, he surprised me by saying, "Yeah, I'm having a hard time breathing myself. I know what you mean."

My jaw dropped.

"And that's another reason why I can't seem to stay away from you—I mean, why you're so addicting. I can read you like a book. It's like—I don't know—it's like we're connected somehow."

So that explains it. I nodded my head in agreement. I decided not to point out that the connection only worked one way, and that it sort of freaked me out. Instead, I grinned and looked down at my fingers as they twisted into the T-shirt I had thrown on after my bubble bath.

Bubble bath! Oh my gosh! I'm not even dressed cute! My hand flew to my head. My hair was still in its messy bun. I didn't even know what my face looked like, since the last time I remembered being fully awake, I was crying. *You've got to be kidding me! I probably look like a monster.*

Tony chuckled and leaned closer to me. "You're beautiful."

I nervously glanced away. "Okay, now I know you're crazy."

"Claire."

I braved a peep at him. He was smiling this totally hot smile. My insides exploded into a gazillion butterflies. *This guy loves me. Me. I can't believe he loves me.*

"Why can't you believe it?"

I didn't freak out this time. It was like I was getting used to him being able to read me. "I don't know. It's like a dream or something, like you can't be real."

He laughed. "I'm real. Didn't today teach you that? Believe me, I'm just as much of a jerk as the next guy." He scrunched his eyes as if remembering.

"No, you're not." I leaned forward and cradled his head in my hands, softly touching his eyelids with my thumbs. The lines erased as his face relaxed. Slowly, my thumbs took on a mind of their own as they explored his eyebrows and the fine hairs of his eyelashes. They were so long. *Guys shouldn't be allowed to have such long eyelashes. It isn't fair.*

"That tickles." Tony grinned, his eyes still closed.

"Sorry," I whispered. I would've removed my hands, but

they wouldn't leave. Instead, my fingers straightened his hair back across his forehead. When I felt how silky soft his hair was, I couldn't help myself. I never wanted to stop touching it. All at once, my fingers were twisting and twirling and dancing in his locks—testing multiple hairstyles on the poor guy. My hands combed and styled and then fluffed it up to start all over again. I had almost forgotten he was there, until—

"That feels so good."

Shocked to hear his voice, I looked down. His eyes twinkled up at me. It looked as if he had been watching me for a little while. My hands stilled in his hair. I grinned and tried to think rationally, but I couldn't. I was caught playing in his hair, for crying out loud. Like I couldn't stand to be apart from him. Like I was just trying to stall before I got up the guts to kiss him. Like I . . . *kiss him? Where did that come from?*

My gaze flew to his mouth and then back up to his eyes again. Nervously, I licked my lips. *Do I have the guts to kiss him?* Technically, I'd never kissed a guy before—they had both kissed me. *Are girls supposed to make the first move? I wish Cass was here to tell me what to do—no, wait! Erase that thought. I do not want her here right now.*

It didn't matter. All of my internal rambling didn't matter, because Tony obviously got tired of waiting. Before I knew what was happening, he wrapped his arms around me and kissed me himself.

I thought I was going to burst.

"Claire! Tony!"

We jerked apart.

Cassidy ran up to us. "You've got to check it out! You're on the news!"

"What?" I gasped. *Oh, no.*

"Are you kidding?" Tony exclaimed. "You are kidding,

right? Tell me you're kidding."

She laughed. "Nope. It's awesome. You've gotta check it out—come on. It looks like someone managed to record you on their camera. Hurry! It's coming up after the next commercial break." With that, she turned and ran back up to the house.

Tony moaned. "This is worse than I thought. I'm on the news? Already? My parents are really gonna freak."

"How much time do we have?" I asked.

He shrugged. "They have a lot of friends. Someone is bound to recognize me. I'm thinking no more than five minutes after it airs, tops."

Oh my gosh! "What are you going to do?"

Tony paused and looked out into the yard, his gaze far away. With a small shake of his head, he answered, "Quit the band. There's not much else I can do now. I was hoping I might be able to convince them that you guys were family, but—but if it's on the news, then they're gonna be . . . it's gonna be bad."

"You can't quit the band. I won't let you. You have to fight for it—"

"Claire, it's not what you think with my parents. They didn't want me to do this to begin with, but they were nice and caved. If they think it's going to hurt me . . . no way. I'm more important to them than my dreams."

"What about Nora? She'd fight for you, wouldn't she?"

"Nora? Oh yeah, she's been arguing about this since it first happened. She's always thought it was dumb to keep it a secret, and she'll still think so. But to my parents, she's just a kid, like me. Don't get me wrong—I totally get where they're coming from. I mean, if this gets out, I won't be able to go anywhere. Seriously, so much for hangin' with my friends. Our band is big. Well, it's huge, bigger than I ever wanted. We're scheduled to go on tour the second I graduate, but already our fans on

MySpace and Friendster and Facebook are hounding us to visit them. So far, it's been easy to stay low, because most people near where I live have known me forever, and since they've never seen me play or anything, they don't expect me to be the lead singer of a band. Sure, I may look like him but I'm not him, you know what I mean?"

It made sense. I still didn't like it. "So this news report . . . what will happen now?"

Tony stood up and held out his hand for me. When I put mine in his, he pulled me out of the swing and slowly up the path, almost like he was hoping to miss the news report altogether.

Denial. It's a beautiful thing.

He sighed. "Our publicist warned us when we first started out that if any media got wind that we were just a group of high school guys, they were going to be all over that. We were going to have a massive media circus on our hands, like paparazzi and everything."

"That's annoying."

"Yeah, tell me about it. Fans like you. They're not out to see if they can catch you doing something stupid, not like the paparazzi, who are always trying to find some story or angle somewhere."

"Well, come on, maybe the news thing won't be that big of a deal," I said. "The image is probably all blurry anyway. Maybe it won't be as bad as you think."

It was worse. Way worse.

"Listen up, all you native Seattleites, have we got a surprise for you. Apparently the elusive Jackson Russolini—front man and lead singer for the popular new band Northanger Alibi—has been spotted in Queen Anne Hill, serenading a girl who looks to be his new girlfriend." Video footage of Tony singing to me flashed across the screen. It looked like it'd been shot from one of the upper windows across the street.

"How do we know this is Jackson Russolini, you ask?"

Another video footage tape popped up, and you could see Tony waving goodbye, grabbing my hand, and escaping into the house with me. The camera switched to Cassidy. She was screaming and jumping up and down, shouting, "Jackson! Jackson! We love you! Northanger Alibi rocks!"

Cassidy groaned and buried her head into an accent pillow on the couch as the screen flipped back to the newscaster.

"And that isn't all—just remember, you heard it first here at King5—it seems that Jackson not only lives among us, and has his whole life, but some of you may know him. His alias is—"

The screen flipped to show Roger. He was beaming proudly into the small camera phone. "Yeah, I know him. My wife and I are good friends with his parents, Ilene and Jonathan. His name is Tony Russo."

No!

"There you have it, folks. Our own Ilene and Jonathan Russo, owners and directors of Northwest Academy, have a rock star for a son. Who knew Jackson lived so close? We certainly didn't! And in other star-studded news, it looks as though—"

I didn't have to hear any more. Tony was standing so stiffly, I wondered if he'd gone into shock. *This is not good.*

Because of his reaction to the news, no one said anything. In fact, after Roger turned down the volume on the TV with the remote, he just nervously sat there. Darlene was curled up next to him, fingering the fringe on the pillow in her lap.

My sister was the only one brave enough to say something. "Sorry, Tony," she said quietly.

He didn't move, just stared ahead, watching the muted screen.

After a couple of seconds, Cassidy mouthed and asked if he

was upset.

I nodded my head.

She mouthed a big "Oh," and turned her head away.

Tony's phone rang.

That was quick!

With a jolt, he jumped back and grabbed the phone from his pocket. It continued to ring as he stared at it. Finally, after a few more seconds, he took a deep breath and answered it. "Hi, Mom. Yeah, I saw the news." He ran his hand through his hair and opened the front door, then quickly shut it.

We could hear people yelling and cheering outside. Cassidy ran to the window and peeked out. "Holy cow!"

"No, Mom, that wasn't anything . . ." Tony paced a moment in the room, and then headed into the kitchen. "Look, she's—No! Mom. I know, okay? I know . . ." He closed the kitchen door behind him.

"Um." Roger cleared his throat. "So, is he in big trouble now? I didn't know—I didn't mean—"

"I know that." I tried to smile to reassure him, but it didn't work.

"Really, we had no idea he was this Jackson guy until today, anyway," Darlene cried from her seat. "Honest—"

"I know. Don't worry about it," I almost snapped. "Look, I didn't know who he was either, okay? He came to tell me. He knew he was going to get in trouble for it—he knew it, and he's prepared to deal with it." *Okay, so not to this extent, but they didn't need to know that.*

"I am really sorry." Cassidy turned from the window. She looked like she was going to cry. "Is this what celebrities have to deal with?" She jabbed her thumb behind her, pointing outside. "It's like the whole neighborhood is out there! How did so many people find out so fast? And the news—how did the news pick it up already?"

Roger smiled ruefully. "Well, you can thank modern technology for that. The Internet is an amazing tool. It probably only took a couple of minutes to download and send that video off to the news station. They obviously didn't waste anytime putting it together." He shook his head. "Poor boy. If I'd have known he was going to go through all that" —he waved toward the TV— "I would've kicked everyone out of the yard."

"I know what you mean." Cassidy groaned. "Could I have been a bigger spaz, seriously?"

I stood up. Their talking was beginning to bug me. *If they were quiet, maybe I could hear what was happening with Tony.*

"Well, I for one thought it was very romantic," Darlene added.

Cassidy gasped. "Oh, I know! I bet Claire—"

I lost it. I walked out of the room and into the kitchen, then shut the door behind me.

TWENTY-TWO
♥
A SAD CRUSH

"Well, I'm willing to make that sacrifice . . ." Tony's back was to me, and he was standing firm. "Yes, she means that much to me—that's why I did it! I know I'll have to quit, okay? I was fully aware of the consequences when I did it." I watched as he paced a moment, staring at the window. "What? No!" he yelled. "Like I set that up for some big publicity stunt. You know, I think you'd be smart enough to realize that. Wait! Look, I'm sorry. I had no idea so many people would witness it. Honest. I didn't even think anyone was there—and I definitely didn't do it because our song is topping the charts—no matter what you think!"

Clearly frustrated, Tony whipped around on his heel. He jolted when he saw me. Our eyes locked, and he took a deep breath and took a step toward me. He held out his arm, and I gratefully walked into his lopsided hug.

I wrapped my arms all the way around him and held on. If I could have given him my strength right then, I would have.

I wished I could go back in time and take all this from him. I could hear his strong heart rapidly beating within his chest. He clung to my shoulder a moment, his whole body vibrating as he answered, “I love her, Mom.” I felt his hand softly trail through my haphazard bun and then down to my shoulder again. He heaved another sigh. “Yes, I know . . . I know . . . Believe me, I definitely didn’t expect this sort of a wakeup call.” He took another deep breath, and I felt him place a kiss on the top of my head.

I smiled a tiny, secret smile.

Tony flinched and tensed up, his whole body going rigid. “Are you sure?” he almost whispered into the phone. His voice was so thick with emotion that I froze too. “Um, okay. That’ll be hard. That’ll be really hard. I don’t think we need to—” He stopped and listened. I closed my eyes and started pleading for some divine help. I hated to feel him experience this because of me—it was stupid.

“Mom, I promise—” His arm came alive, and he began to rub my shoulder. “Look. It doesn’t have to be . . . there has to be something else. Okay, fine . . . fine. I give up. Does Dad want this?” His hand stopped. “All right. Fine. Give me a call when you know something . . . okay . . . okay. It might be awhile before I can get home . . . Yeah, they’re outside. The whole place is packed . . . I know. I’m sorry. I hate it too. Mom, don’t cry—come on, Mom! Don’t cry. Look, I’m really sorry, okay? . . . Okay, get your other phone . . . Love you too. Bye.”

Tony ended the call. With a huge breath, he wrapped his other arm around me, and we stood together silently for a full minute before he commented into my hair, “Man, this bites. Why doesn’t anybody talk about the bad stuff that goes with being a celebrity?”

I hesitated a moment before I asked, “What’s going on?”

He let out another sigh and pulled me in closer. "I guess the news was announced over the intercom at school right after it was broadcast. The whole faculty knows now. Mom's really upset by it, too. Her phone's already ringing off the hook—everyone's congratulating her and asking for my autograph. My mom's kind of shy around strangers, and this sort of thing really stresses her."

"I'm sorry," I said softly.

"Yeah, well, I never thought about what would happen to my family if word got out. I guess I know now. My dad's already talking about heightened security for us everywhere—my school, the university, definitely the house—it looks like it's going to get bad."

Oh my gosh!

"There is good news, though. They're willing to discuss me staying in the band."

What? I gasped and pulled back a bit so I could see him. He didn't look happy.

"Personally, I think they're crazy, but my mom may have a point. I mean, I can definitely see it from her side."

"See what from her side?"

He chuckled suddenly and grinned down at me. "She's worried about a rebellion."

"Rebellion?"

"Yeah." He shrugged. "Apparently we're bigger than she thought we were. I mean, by the evidence outside, it would seem Northanger Alibi is pretty popular."

"Well, yeah. Hello? You've written—wait a minute! You wrote that song, didn't you?"

Tony nodded like it was no big deal. "Yep. I wrote them all."

Holy cow! "Anyway, of course you're huge. I usually only

listen to country—with a little bit of rock and pop—but this song has totally got me hooked. It's really, really good. So what's the deal? Why a rebellion?"

"Not from me or the band. She thinks the fans may start a riot if they pull me out. You know—hate mail, phone calls, eggs thrown at the house—that sort of thing."

I gasped again. "Would people really do that?"

"I don't know. Depends on how mad they are, I guess. Personally, I think it would be harder for my parents to face paparazzi everywhere than a few angry fans."

"But what if you told everyone it was your choice to leave the band?"

Tony got quiet for a moment, and he watched me. "Do you want me to leave?"

No. "Do you want this life?" I asked him, uncertain what he was thinking.

"I'm happiest when I play. But I can play anywhere."

"Yeah, but who'll be there to hear you?"

His phone rang, and I stepped back as he answered it. "Hello? Oh, hey, Coach. What's up? Is the game still on?"

I grinned as I watched Tony listen. His hair was a bit messed from all the times he'd run his fingers through it. I stood up on tiptoe to straighten it, but Tony stepped back from me, his hand raised in a cautionary gesture.

My eyes flew to his. Something was happening.

He closed his eyes and nodded. "Okay. Thanks for letting me know. All right. Bye." He muttered something under his breath as he hung up the phone. "Well, that was great. Awesome, actually." He looked like he felt far from awesome.

"Now what?"

He tried to chuckle, but it came out as a snort. "I just got fired from volunteering at the Y."

"What? Are you kidding? Why?" *Oh my gosh! He loves those kids!*

Tony looked like he wanted to throw something. I had never seen him so hurt and upset at the same time. "It appears that due to my elevated status" —he held the phone up to look at it and shook his head— "I pose an unnecessary risk to the children." He closed his eyes again. "I'm kindly asked not to come back, or to come to any games."

"Tony, they can't do that! They can't! Why is everyone freaking out about this? I don't get it. They're treating you like you have some sort of disease."

He tried to grin but failed miserably. He tugged me back to his chest. "You look like you want to kick the coach's butt."

"I do!" I stomped my foot. "You have no idea."

Tony chuckled and then sighed. "Man, I'm gonna miss those kids." He paused a moment and then sighed again. "But you're wrong about one thing." He slowly rubbed my back as his voice went quiet. "I do have a disease. It's called fame."

"Tony, I'm so sorry," I whispered.

By the time he left, it was well after midnight. Even then, there were camera crews all over the place. I made the mistake of waving goodbye to him from the door.

Of course I didn't realize it was a mistake until the next morning when pictures of me, still in my messy bun, were splattered all over the newspapers. By the time I came down the stairs at eight o'clock, there'd already been four or five reporters knocking on the door for interviews and about half a dozen phone calls. Everyone wanted to know who I was. This was something I hadn't thought about, but being the girlfriend of a high-profile celebrity was serious news, apparently.

I jumped when the phone started ringing the second I put bread in the toaster. Without saying a word, Roger walked over and calmly ripped the cable out of the wall. He then walked back over to the couch and flipped the channels. King5 was reporting live during their morning show.

"So, who is this mystery girl who has stolen Seattle's Jackson Russolini's heart?" A picture of me waving goodbye was splattered onto the screen. "We don't know, but it seems as though he may have lost more than his heart to her. Jackson was seen leaving her house in the early hours of the morning, folks. And doesn't she look pleased that he stayed so long? Of course, wouldn't you, if you were her?"

Ugh! I thought I was going to scream.

The screen switched to video footage of Tony arriving at his house last night and being bombarded by microphones and cameras. "As we reported yesterday, Tony Russo, the son of the directors of the Northwest Academy, Ilene and Jonathan Russo, is also front man to the new teen band Northanger Alibi. Sources say that Tony, aka Jackson Russolini, has been keeping a low profile here in Seattle for some time. They say he grew up here and has, until recently, been the assistant coach for a soccer team—"

Roger switched the TV off, and I blinked back to life. My cell rang, and I was happy to hear Tony's deep voice on the other end.

"Hey, you. How are ya hangin' in there?" he asked.

"Um, I could be better." I pulled out my almost-cold toast and started buttering. "But other than that, I'm okay. You?"

Tony chuckled. "Missing you."

Aw! "Me too. Want to come over and make me better?"

"Yes, but I can't. I'm calling to let you know I have a flight scheduled for takeoff in about two hours, but I promise I'll stop by the second I get back in."

"What? Where are you going? When will you get back?"

"I've got an appointment with my agent and publicist—they want to decide what to do with this. Plus, it looks like my record producer wants to talk to me about making more music videos since my cover's blown and we're such a hot topic right now. They want to release them while there's still a buzz."

"Oh. And your parents? Are they—are they okay with everything?"

"Yeah, right. No, I mean, they still love me, but they're mad. Their phone hasn't stopped ringing since yesterday. Someone had the nerve to call at three o'clock this morning. They're taking it pretty hard, but they're adamant that I stay in the band as of right now and go to California. So I guess that's a relief—well, sort of. Kind of like a double-edged sword."

I tried to sound brave, but I really didn't want to be left in Seattle alone. I know he didn't mean it that way, but that's exactly what was happening. "Well, that's good for you, though." I cleared my throat and put brightness in my voice when I asked, "So, any tips on fending off the paparazzi?"

Tony chuckled. "I wish I had some. I don't."

"Is there something you wish I wouldn't talk about? Something you don't want me to say—or reveal?"

He hesitated for a minute and then mumbled, "You know, I've been hiding so long that as hard as this is, it's nice to have it all out in the open now. I don't think there's anything you can say that'll hurt me, or freak me out or anything. So, just go with what you're comfortable saying. I totally understand if you want to deny ever knowing me—now *that* I understand—but as far as we're concerned, this is all up to you. I already made my stand to the world when I came to your house yesterday, and I'm still happy with that decision. I always will be, because no matter what happens, I'm so grateful I was able to show you how much you mean to me."

A huge wave of relief washed over me. I was happy to hear that he didn't have any regrets. It was the most awesome feeling in the world to still be loved. In fact— "Tony?"

"Yeah?"

I took a deep breath, closed my eyes, and whispered, "I love you."

He inhaled sharply. "Are you serious? Did I just hear you right?"

I grinned into the phone and turned around. "Yeah, I love you, Tony Russo."

"Sweet!" he hollered. "When I get back, we are so celebrating!"

I giggled. "Have a good time—miss me forever."

Tony paused and then said, "Come with me. I'm serious, come with me. Come to California. Have you ever been?"

"What? No. I've never been."

"You'll love it. Say you'll come!"

My heart pounded in my chest with excitement before I mentally pictured my mom's face. "I would love to, but my mom would kill me. Then she'd kill Cass, then Darlene and Roger, and then she'd probably come after you, too."

Tony sighed. "Ah, well, if she's going to go after everyone, then I better not push it. I mean, if it was just me, I'd say come anyway—but to jeopardize everyone else, I guess I'll just wait until I get home. Text me your e-mail addy, okay? I want to shoot you e-mails and texts and everything else."

"Okay. I will as soon as we hang up."

"All right, I'm outta here so you won't forget. I love you, Claire Hart. Take care, and don't maim anyone unless they deserve it, okay?"

I giggled. "I never do!"

"Well, at least wait until I can be there to watch. I need to know what methods you use."

"Bye!" I rolled my eyes.

"Bye." He chuckled just before I heard the phone click.

I love you.

TWENTY-THREE
♥
THE FINAL BLOW

"What do you mean you've got an interview with King5?" I nearly hollered into the phone at Jaden. "Why are they interviewing you, anyway? You hardly even know me!"

"Not *going to* interview me, *did* interview me. And why are you freaking out? I'm your best friend, remember? I figured they'd want to hear your side of the story."

What in the—? "Jaden, are you for real? You don't even *know* my side of the story! You're messin' with me, right? You've called me up to play a joke on me, because I know there's no way you've gone and done an interview about me—posing as my stupid best friend—on live TV. Even you wouldn't be that stupid. So, ha ha. Joke's over. You can come clean now."

"Come on. What's got your panties all twisted, anyway? It was no big deal—all they wanted to know was some of the things you're interested in—you know, that sort of thing."

"Shut up! You really did an interview today?" *I'm gonna kill him! I'm gonna string him up across some live wires and—*

"What is the big deal? The lady was nice—and hot, by the way. She really wanted to know about you, so I just opened up and told her a few things."

My voice grew ice cold. "Like what?" *He better not have said anything about kissing me—*

"Oh, I don't know." I could almost hear the shrug. "I told them that you like Old Navy, Orange Julius smoothies, *Twilight*—you know, that type of thing."

"You are such a dork, you know that? A total dork! Why'd you bring up *Twilight*? What has that got to do with anything?"

"I don't know. You like it."

"Look, tell me everything you said. I want every word."

"Nope."

"No? No?" Okay, now I was really gonna strangle him. "What do you mean no?"

"I mean, you gotta see the interview yourself. It'll be on later tonight."

"Jaden, you better have only said extremely wonderful things about me, or I'm gonna—"

"Yeah, yeah, I know, you'll kick my butt." He chuckled as though this were all a game. "So, uh, when you see how great I did—and since it's all over the papers that your boyfriend won't be back for a couple of weeks—you wanna thank me with a kiss?"

"Jaden, seriously. Get a life."

"Why?" He chuckled. "Watching you try to live yours is way more exciting."

I muttered a series of unintelligible words, sounding more like a Tasmanian devil than an actual human being, but I didn't care. *Jaden is so going down.*

"You know you're cute when you're mad." He laughed again.

I nearly threw the phone. Instead, I took a deep breath and

vowed to find the positive in this situation. "Okay, okay, look. You're right. I'm not going to freak out unless there's a reason." I took another deep breath while he chuckled in my ear. "You just better not have given me any reason to flip out, you got that?"

"Man, get over it. Everything will be perfect, you'll see."

{♥}

Later that night, I wished I'd had the foresight to invite Jaden over—that way, he'd be right next to me when my fury broke loose. Which it did, right about the time Jaden told the pretty newswoman I thought he was a werewolf when I first met him. Oh yeah, they both had a good long laugh about that. It was so hilarious, you have no idea. Even Roger and Darlene thought it was funny and joined in. Only Cassidy looked a little freaked out and even slightly worried for me.

I didn't understand the extent of her stress until Jaden announced, "Yeah, that's not all. She totally thought Tony was a vampire, too, just like Edward in those Twilight books. I'm serious. She really, really did—she thought he could read her mind and everything!"

Oh. My. Gosh. I couldn't breathe. I couldn't think. And just when I thought it couldn't get any worse, he continued, "Yeah, the only way she found out he wasn't a vampire was when he kissed her!" He chuckled obnoxiously. "Can you imagine her shock when she realized his lips were warm instead of cold?"

Roger and Darlene burst into more laughter. She looked like she was about to have a seizure, she was laughing so hard.

My head began to buzz, and my vision was starting to fade. One quick glance at Cassidy and I knew she was as sickly stunned as I was. Without saying a word, I scrambled off the couch and ran up the stairs to my room.

This can't be happening to me! Oh my gosh! This can't be happening! I wondered briefly how long I'd actually have before Tony heard about the news story. He was going to freak out—I knew it. I took a deep breath and willed myself not to have a heart attack. Too late. My vision only became more blurry and my breathing more labored. In fact, I wondered briefly if I was going to pass out again. Then I felt my cheeks grow wet, which was almost a relief because crying was way better than fainting, in my opinion.

After kicking off my shoes, I curled up on the bed. Was this ever going to get any better?

About ten minutes later, I learned it wasn't getting better any time soon. My cell phone rang. *Dang. What if it's Tony?*

It wasn't. It was Nora.

"Hey, Claire?" She sounded uncomfortable and nervous. It was the first time I'd spoken to her since the mall incident.

"Yeah?"

"Um, my dad wants to talk to you. Is that okay?"

Her dad? Tony's dad? What does he *want?* "Um, okay." I tried to take the scared tone out of my voice when he picked up, but it didn't work. I was terrified. "What can I do for you?"

"Claire." He heaved a sigh into the phone. I knew before he spoke that it wasn't going to be good. "Ilene and I have been talking it over, and we've come to the conclusion that you should head back to Farmington."

What? "Why?"

"We feel it would be in the best interest of everyone involved if you did."

"But—but I don't understand."

"Anthony won't be thrilled to hear that you've been calling him a vampire. In fact, knowing Tony's aversion to anything vampire related, we suggest you leave before he finds out. We are only thinking of you, and even though the image of our son has been greatly hurt because of your dealings with him, we feel that if you go now, he may have a chance to rebuild what little of his character he has left."

"I don't know what to say . . ."

"If you truly love Tony, you would've already said that you're leaving. The fact that we're discussing the issue this long tells me you're only concerned about yourself and not him at all."

"That's not true!" *I love him.*

"Then prove it and leave. If you're out of the state, and he comes to visit you, the media won't get wind of it. Farmington is a lot smaller than Seattle. Tony could probably hide much better there. With you still here, nothing will ever die down—it'll just be a continuous mass of confusion."

I could actually see where he was coming from. "But what about Darlene and Roger? He isn't finished with his training."

Jonathan Russo sighed into the phone again. "His training has been put on hold anyway. There's no way he can show up at the college right now—there are people everywhere waiting to get a glimpse of anyone who knows Tony. Look, I wanted to give you a heads-up. We will be speaking to Roger about this shortly. I'm just hoping you can do the wise and mature thing and leave without a fuss. Tony's whole life has been disrupted since meeting you, and now with this gruesome vampire story, it's only going to get worse. The media is already laughing at you two like this was the biggest joke in history. Can you imagine how much more damage it will do to his career if you stay? Do you even have any idea how much that boy has risked for you as it is?"

"Probably not. I mean, I have an idea, but probably nothing compared to the whole story. I'm sorry about the vampire thing.

I—I didn't know it was going to become public knowledge."

"Well, welcome to the world of celebrity, the world from which we have tried to shield our son. It's vicious and brutal, and only cares about getting viewers and making money. Feelings don't count." Jonathan groaned. When he spoke again, he sounded about twenty years older. "Poor Ilene has not been taking this well. This media circus has not helped her at all. In fact, the stress has been . . . Uh, look, I don't know why I'm talking to you about this. I need to get a hold of Roger now. I hope you will take our suggestion to heart and not put up a fuss, okay?"

"Uh, sure. I promise to think about it."

"You do that."

The phone clicked in my ear. For a good ten minutes I just sat there, absorbing everything he'd said. As much as I hated to admit it, Tony's dad was right. With an exhausted moan, I walked over to the closet and pulled out my suitcase. Maybe it was time I got out of Seattle anyway. The whole celebrity thing was way more than a typical sixteen-year-old could cope with.

While I was emptying my side of the dresser, Cassidy came up to tell me Mom was on the phone. The look my sister gave me spoke volumes. It'd only been three days since Tony had sung to me under the balcony, but it felt more like thirty.

I sighed, placed my hand over the receiver, and pointed to the dresser. "Better start packing. Jonathan Russo is calling Roger now to convince us all to leave."

Cassidy nodded. "Figures." She didn't even blink. She just walked over to the closet and grabbed her suitcase. By the time I said hello into the phone, she had already began to pack.

"I want you home, right now!" Mom declared. "What in the world has been going on, anyway? The last time we talked, everything was perfect, and now this!"

"Look, Mom—" I didn't have the heart to really protest.

"No, *you* look! I have to find out on the cover of a tabloid that my daughter is sleeping with some rock star!"

What? Holy cow! "No way, Mom! Not even! That's just the stupid tabs lying. You have to believe me."

My mom snorted in the phone. I heard her hand move across the mouthpiece as though she were muffling it.

"Mom? You do believe me, right?"

All pretense gone, Mom cracked up and removed her hand. "Duh, I totally believe you."

"You know, you could've told me you were just messing with me." I crammed a couple more shirts in the suitcase. "It hasn't been exactly easy around here the last couple of days."

"It's a good thing I know you'd never do anything like that. It's the only reason your butt isn't getting busted right now. Still doesn't make it easy to read. Thank goodness they don't have all the details—and that picture was blurry—or we'd be getting hounded right now."

"Well, count yourself lucky. Seattle has been buzzing like their nose hair is on fire since Tony first came and sang to me."

"Tony? As in the friend of the Hadleys? I thought the paper was saying his name was Johnson or Justin or something—"

"Jackson is his middle name. He goes by that when he's playing, so no one knows who he is."

My mom didn't seem too interested. Instead she asked, "So missy, what are your plans now that you've left your mark on Seattle? Are you planning to descend on Portland next?" She chuckled.

It was a relief to hear that she was amused. At least someone could see the ridiculous side of this whole thing. "No, I think I've done enough damage for one summer. I'll save Portland for next year. I'm coming home."

"When?"

"Well, Tony's dad is hoping the sooner the better. He's talking to Roger right now, so it looks like it'll probably be tomorrow."

"Ah." Mom snorted. "Yep, their son must have it bad. I can see why they'd want you out of there as soon as possible. What does he say about all of this?"

"Who? Tony's dad?"

"No. Tony."

"Oh, he's in California right now, with his agent and publicist and record label. They're trying to figure out some way to use all the publicity to their advantage. Tony has called me a few times since he left, and e-mailed and texted me."

"And? What's he saying?"

"Oh!" I blushed. *That I'm the most wonderful girl in the whole world, and he loves me like crazy.* Of course, that's what he was saying about me before tonight's vampire episode. "Ugh!"

"He's saying ugh?" my mom teased.

"No." I chuckled. "He's saying all the right Prince Charming sorts of things he should. You'd really like him. I mean, he did go ahead and stick around, even after your stupid Dating Ritual. Thanks a lot for that—it was humiliating!"

My mom started laughing hard. "You liked that, did you? Hee hee hee! I knew you'd get a kick out of it."

"Ha ha." Mom's idea of "kicks" and mine were not even on the same planet.

"Well, hurry home. Call me when you find out what's going on, okay?"

"Sure, Mom. I will."

"M'kay. Love you."

"Love you too, Mom. Bye."

TWENTY-FOUR
♥
HOME SWEET HOME

Twenty-four hours later, our plane landed in New Mexico. It was kind of rough dodging the paparazzi in Seattle, but with Tony's family to distract them, we were able to pull it off. That's all I needed—someone tailing me to Farmington.

Mom and Dad were waiting for us and had a large meal on the dining room table when we walked in. It was such a comfort to come home to enchiladas after the ordeal we'd been through. Even Cass, who'd spent the flight finishing the last book in the Twilight series, was eager to just relax at home.

As soon as I could, I ran to an outlet and plugged in my cell. It had run out of power halfway through our trip, and I hadn't heard back from Tony yet. I'd sent him a text last night saying we were heading home, and since it'd been almost twenty-four hours, I expected there to be a text waiting for me.

While the battery was charging and the messages loading, I filled up my plate and sat down to eat with the family. Cassidy and I were bombarded with questions about Seattle and our trip home. I answered as best I could, skipping over all the kisses I'd gotten. I might tell my mom later in her room or something, just between us. Instead, I used the opportunity to paint Tony in a wonderful light so my parents would give him the chance he deserved. I made sure to talk about his soccer team and his incredible musical talent, and also how nice he was and how much he loved kids. I think by the time I was done, even the curtains were in love with the guy.

"Wow." Mom chuckled. "He sounds like a perfect boyfriend."

"Well, I for one can't wait to meet him," my dad said. "Let us know when he plans on headin' this way."

I giggled at the thought of Tony coming here. *Oh my gosh—Tony!* I jumped up to check my cell and see what he'd said.

There were no messages from him.

Huh?

There were, however, a couple of "I'm so sorry" texts from Jaden, but I just skimmed over those. Even my e-mail inbox was suspiciously empty. I tried not to let it bug me while I helped clear the table.

By the time I finished loading the dishwasher, I'd already come up with six or seven good excuses why Tony hadn't texted, or e-mailed, or anything.

But three hours later as I was climbing into bed, I began to doubt those excuses completely. Instead, I found myself facing the reality that something could be seriously wrong. I didn't like that reality. I would much prefer to think happy thoughts as long as I possibly could, until proven differently.

Except that's the thing. Since the day we went to the movies together, Tony had never gone a full day without contacting me somehow, and with the rising media and craziness in our lives, he'd been really good about touching base at least two or three times a day. Just not *this* day—the day after Jaden announced in an exclusive interview that I thought Tony was a vampire.

I was worried. Okay, so I was more than worried. I was downright terrified that Tony hated me. He'd made it pretty clear that the thought of vampires creeped him out—even his family knew that, so he must've been really vocal about it.

I tried to keep my rising panic at bay as I typed out another text that night. It wasn't easy.

> Hey u, got hme safe. miss u like
> crzy. wsh u were here. luv, me

By the time I pushed the "send" button, I was gasping for breath. I knew I was totally being melodramatic, but I couldn't help it. The thought that Tony hated me was more than I could bear. Never mind the fact that we'd had an extra-dramatic relationship to begin with—all this drama was killing me. I needed reassurance—a lot of reassurance—and no one was there to give it to me. All I wanted to do was say I was sorry. I really couldn't explain much, because, well, what Jaden had said was the truth. So it wasn't like I had a million good excuses for why I'd thought it. I just wished Jaden hadn't said anything to begin with. Not that it would've changed anything. I'd thought Tony was a stupid vampire until just a few days ago.

Why was I ever so blind? Could there be a bigger dork than me anywhere?

Clutching my phone, I pulled the covers up over my head and lay there, trying to will myself into breathing normally. When Cassidy knocked on my door a little while later, I pretended I was asleep. The last thing I needed was my sister bugging me about Tony.

I couldn't sleep, though. As much as I pretended to, and

later even wanted to, I couldn't. Instead, my eyes watched the clock on my phone, waiting for Tony to answer me, while my mind replayed over and over again all the moments we'd had together.

9:51

10:07

11:26

12:33

1:18

2:42

3:02

I finally zonked out sometime after four.

Five mornings later, I realized this was becoming a late-night ritual. I groaned. Then I rolled over in my bed and looked at my alarm clock. It was ten forty-five! *Sheesh!* I jumped out of the covers and searched frantically for my phone. When I found it, the battery was almost dead because I'd used the light so much the night before. Scanning quickly, I could see there were still no texts from Tony. It had been a week. A whole week and I still hadn't heard from him.

In dejection, I tossed the phone on my desk and curled up

in bed again. No one even bothered to check on me for at least another hour. I tried to use that to my advantage and sleep some time away, but it wouldn't work. My happy memories were replaced with mean, angry imaginings.

I was positive Tony hated me. I was positive he was mad—really mad. His silence was more ominous than any tear-jerking letter he could've sent. It was the most horrible, cruel way to treat someone. Especially someone like me, who used words for everything. Even when my friend Emma had railed on me in front of a whole Christmas party full of people—that didn't hurt as much as this did. And that was saying a lot, because eighteen months ago, I thought that was the worst thing I could've ever gone through. Now, I would take Emma chewing me out eight times over one silent Tony any day.

Just tell me off, already! I get it. I'm a horrible person who's completely naive and gullible and prefers living in an imaginary world more than reality.

Except that wasn't who I was anymore. I wasn't the same Claire Hart who'd traveled to Seattle. I was different and more mature and everything. I just needed a chance to prove that to Tony.

How can I be given that chance when he won't even acknowledge me? Who am I trying to kid, anyway?

I sat up in bed and pushed down the covers.

Tony Russo is a rock star, for crying out loud! A huge, highly paid rock star who has loads of girls throwing themselves at his feet. He doesn't need me. And if I'd actually think about it and listen to his parents, I'd see what he must see—that I'm bad for his career. I mean, isn't it a law or something that when a band starts out, it's really good for the singers to be single? I'm sure I've heard that somewhere.

I tried to think about it for a minute and make that thought work into my subconscious, except all it did was remind me of every famous singer I knew who was either married or going out with someone.

Okay, maybe he got a girlfriend while he was in Cali? Um, okay, that hurt. Let's come up with something else. Oh, I know! Maybe he can't have a girlfriend right now. Maybe it's part of his contract with his company to not talk to me . . . hmm . . . Okay, so knowing Tony like I do, probably not. He'd consider it a challenge and purposely fling our relationship in their faces.

Okay, calm down. I'm dreaming again. Tony is just a guy. A seventeen-year-old guy who is technically a minor and basically has to do whatever he's told—within reason. Well, he's a smart guy, so hopefully they were able to discuss things enough to see that—

"Hey, Claire? Are you up?" It was Mom.

"Yeah, I'm up. Give me a sec to get dressed, and I'll come out."

"Okay. I've been a bit worried about you. You've been moping for days now and sleeping way too long each morning. I mean, it is almost eleven-thirty. Are you okay? Is there something you want to talk about?"

"Yeah, yeah. I mean, no. I'm fine. I'm just tired. I'll be out in a sec." I grudgingly crawled off the bed and threw on a pair of jeans and my favorite comfy vintage Holly Hobby T-shirt. Then I looked in my full-length mirror and grumbled. *Dang! I look like the bride of Frankenstein.*

I grabbed a wide-tooth comb and worked it through a ton of knots, the marvelous product of another sleepless night. My face was haggard as well, and I knew my mom was going to ask me a million questions. So I quickly slapped on some makeup, and it worked. I looked a hundred times better. After I pulled my comfy flip-flops out of the closet, I stuck a piece of gum in my mouth so my mom wouldn't force me to eat anything. I really wasn't in the mood for breakfast.

With a sigh and a plastered smile on my face, I opened the door and gasped.

Tony was leaning against the wall across from my room, with one leg up and his hands in his pockets.

"Hello, beautiful."

TWENTY-FIVE

A NEW DAWN BREAKS

"Tony! When? How? What in the world—is it really you?" I knew I was smiling like a dork, but I didn't care.

He grinned at my confusion and pushed himself off the wall, taking a step toward me. "Just for the record, a week is way too long to go without seeing you."

"Really?" *Eeeh!*

"Claire?" He took another step forward and closed the distance in the little hallway.

"Yeah?" I gazed into his glittering eyes. *I can't believe he's really here!*

"You're smiling. Smiling is good." He brought the back of his hand up to gently caress my cheek with his knuckles. "I didn't know if I'd ever get to see your smile again—if I'd ever deserve it."

"What do you mean? I'll always smile when you're around."

His sad eyes searched mine a moment. The tension and

wariness on his features called for me to reach out and hug him—but I didn't. I waited.

"Claire, I'm so sorry my family treated you the way they did. I should've seen it coming. I should've realized they would try something like this the second I left. I can't believe you're even talking to me." I was extremely distracted by his knuckles trailing on my cheek.

My hand reached up to still his. Very slowly, I moved it away and entwined our fingers together. "You're not your dad. I know that."

"But, Claire—"

"I also know that your dad was right."

Tony's eyes flashed. "No. He was wrong."

I shook my head. "You were humiliated during an interview. All of Seattle watched Jaden announce that I thought you were a vampire—"

"And then it was syndicated, and most of the Southwest picked it up and viewed it."

"What?" My knees went weak.

Tony wrapped his free hand around my waist and propped me up before I'd even realized what had happened.

"Are you kidding me?" I was fully conscious of him being so close to me. My breathing was starting to go funny again.

"Claire." He wrapped me up close to his heart and whispered, "I wasn't humiliated. I promise." I felt him lean forward and kiss the top of my head and then mutter, "You were."

I closed my eyes and relaxed into his comforting chest. *He's right. I was. I was so humiliated.*

"You were the only one hurt by what Jaden did. I've never wanted to strangle someone more in my life than I did when I watched that interview in my hotel room. It's a real good thing he wasn't anywhere near me. I'd heard about the interview and what he said, and I was already mad about it. But seeing him smirk and laugh, I could've gladly become the vampire you wanted me to be and torn that wolf limb from limb."

I giggled into Tony's shirt. I couldn't help it. He was so upset, and it was so cute.

He groaned and released my hand to wrap his other arm around me. "And then my dad calling you, after you'd just gone through that—I was so mad. Seriously, when my dad explained in detail what had happened, first on the show and then what he'd done to you, thinking I'd be happy—man, I lost it. It was like everything I'd wanted to say for the past few years all came boiling out."

Oh, no. I pulled back a little to see Tony better. "What happened?"

"Dang! You're so hot when you're worried," he whispered down at me.

"Really?"

"How did I ever get so lucky to find you?"

I grinned for a moment and then asked seriously, "Why didn't you call?" *Or text? Or email? Or send a smoke signal? Anything?*

Tony bit his lip and closed his eyes. He leaned forward until his forehead gently touched mine and whispered, "I was afraid."

What? "Why? What do you—oh, because of your dad?"

"Yeah. Well, that and I couldn't stand it if you told me you never wanted to see me again. I figured the best defense was nothing."

"So you didn't call me? For a whole week?" A little perturbed, I stepped away from him.

"I figured it was better to see you in person and explain than it was to hear you tell me off on the phone."

"So instead, you made me suffer? And stress and worry and go crazy for days, wondering if you hated me?"

Tony's eyes sparkled. "Did you really go crazy worrying about me?"

I put my hands on my hips. "Do you think this is funny?"

He chuckled and slipped his hands through my elbows, then wrapped his arms around my waist again. "Has anyone ever told you you're cute when you're mad?"

Instantly, Jaden flashed through my mind, and I jerked away. I knew I was overreacting and wasn't thinking rationally, but it was like my body had taken on a mind of its own. *We need space,* I thought. I tilted my chin up and walked past him into the small living room we reserved for guests. When I turned around, ready to do battle, I saw that Tony was still in the same spot in the hallway. His arms were folded across his chest, and his grin was really beginning to grate on my nerves.

"So, is this what the werewolf had to deal with?" he asked teasingly.

"The werewolf? Of all the—!"

"Oh, don't mind Claire," my mom said as she entered the room. "She's always been a bit high maintenance."

Good grief. "I have not, Mom! For crying out loud, where did that come from?"

"See what I mean?" she called over to Tony and then waved her hand, beckoning him to come into the room. "Don't worry, though. Her bark is way sharper than her bite."

"Interesting metaphor." He chuckled as he sauntered into the room. "If I didn't know better, I'd wonder if she was a vampire, or a werewolf."

I glared. He smiled.

"So, Tony," Mom interrupted. "I didn't really get a chance to talk to you earlier. I'd love to get to know you. How about we chat while Claire's eating in the kitchen?" My mom sat down on the couch and gave me the "leave now" look.

"Sure." He shrugged and then promptly sat down on the chair across from her. "What do you want to know?"

I frowned. "Are you kidding?"

Tony and my mom both blinked at me.

I rolled my eyes. "Fine, get to know him. Just remember, he came here to see *me.*"

"See what I mean?" Mom smiled. "High maintenance. Now go eat your breakfast, dear."

As if I am ten years old. Grr. Put in my way "overly reactive" place, I marched into the kitchen and tried to eat something.

Knowing my mom, she was probably giving him the third degree, and that made me vengefully happy. *Good! Tony needs to go through something painful.* After I tossed my gum, I grabbed an apple and started munching. I can't believe he didn't call me. *The punk!* In disgust, I slumped down on the stool by the counter.

"Oh. My. Gosh!" Cassidy said as she skittered into the kitchen. "Is that Jackson with Mom in the living room?"

"Yeah," I grumbled.

"Holy back-flippin' cow! When did he get here?" I watched as she glanced at her reflection in the double-oven door and ran her fingers through her hair.

"I don't know." I took another bite. "Gee, Cass. You don't have to get that excited about it."

"Are you kidding me?" She flipped around and stared at me hard. "What's got you all snippety?"

"Just that he's—"

"You know what? I don't want to know what it was. If you don't want that guy, just tell me now."

My jaw dropped, and a piece of apple fell out of my

mouth.

"Eew." She grimaced.

"What about Ethan?" I asked, shocked that she was even interested in Tony.

"Um, 'kay. Claire?" Cassidy acted like I was two. "Jackson Russolini is in our house. *In our house.* To see you. YOU! And, um, in case you haven't noticed, the guy is hot—like seriously hot. I don't care who you are or who you're going with, you'd dump him if Jackson was looking twice at you."

"Are you nuts? I wouldn't."

It was her turn to look shocked. "You're actually serious? You wouldn't dump your boyfriend to go out with Jackson?"

"No." I looked at her with a sneer. "I don't actually base my opinion of guys on who they are. It's more on how they act."

Cassidy put her hands on her hips. "Please. And what has Jackson done to you, anyway?"

"Well, he didn't—"

"Oh, wait! I know. Was it him leaving California early to come and check on you that made you mad?"

"What? No. It was—"

"Or was it the extra-expensive tickets he had to buy just to get a last-minute flight?"

"Whatever." I looked away from her.

"Or . . . ooh! Maybe it was the hours he spent in layovers that got you upset?"

She's never going to get it. Ever. I dropped my head into my hands.

Cassidy walked up to the counter and said quietly, "Possibly it was the surprise appearance he made at your house to let you know in person how much he loves you. Would you rather he just texted you from Cali, then?"

"Leave me alone, Cass," I mumbled into my arms.

"You know what? You don't know a good thing when you've got it." Her voice rose. "I'm serious! Any girl would *kill* to have Jackson Russolini in her house with her, and instead you're in here, sulking in the kitchen."

I lifted my head. "I'm not sulk—"

"Whatever. You're not even worthy enough to be Jackson's girlfriend."

"I don't want to be Jackson's girlfriend!" I snapped. "I don't even want Jackson, okay? I want Tony. TONY! That's the guy I'm in love with. Yeah, Jackson's cool and all, but he's nothing. He's a shell, Cassidy, like Edward—fake! Tony is real, and he's amazing, and he cares about things and people, but mostly he cares if people see him for who he really is. I can't believe—"

I felt large, warm arms wrap around my shoulders and pull me back into a firm chest. "Which is why I don't deserve you." His deep voice surrounded my head.

With a gasp, I watched as Cassidy forced her mouth closed.

"I'm sorry you were worried." Tony kissed the top of my head. "I'm sorry you suffered." I felt another kiss on my head—closer to my brow this time. "I'm sorry you stressed over me."

I smiled softly as Tony's hands captured each side of my face and tilted my head back. I closed my eyes. He pressed his lips to the middle of my forehead and then huskily whispered, "I'm sorry I made you go crazy for days wondering if I hated you." He kissed my forehead again. "I don't hate you." He kissed the tip of my nose. "I love you." He tilted my head farther back, cradling it with his chest and hands. "Do you know why I love you?"

Grinning, I shook my head slightly, my eyes still closed.

"I love you because you're ornery and tough and funny and imaginative and sweet and caring and real. But mostly I love you because you love me. The real me." Then his lips caught mine—my nose skimming his chin—in the most romantic, un-book-like kiss ever.

My heart melted, and I smiled big as he pulled away.

Cassidy cleared her throat. "Ahem. So, um, I'm gonna head out of here. You two, uh, carry on without me, okay?"

Tony and I both laughed as he released my head, and I twisted around in my seat to see him better.

"Sorry," I said to Cass, but I was practically giggling up at my guy.

"Yeah, yeah, I can tell you're as remorseful as you can be," she muttered as she made her exit.

I liked the way Tony's eyes continued to roam over my face, never once looking at my sister. After she'd left, my eyes locked with his, and I said quietly, "Forgiven."

It was as if a whole weight of worry flew from his shoulders. He took a deep breath and shook his head. "What am I going to do with you?"

I bit my lip and peeked flirtatiously up at him from under my eyelashes. "Uh, kiss me again?"

"Done." He leaned forward and set another swift kiss on my lips. "But I didn't mean that. I meant, what am I going to do when I'm with you every day?"

What? "With me every day? What are you saying?"

He grinned and put his hands in his pockets, focusing on his shoes a moment before bringing his gaze back up at me. "I'm saying that my family has debated retiring early and moving from Seattle to a smaller town, to escape the press and gain some sanity again."

Huh?

"I was told to look around and choose somewhere quiet to live."

"Oh my gosh! Are you saying what I think you're saying?" I stood up.

"Yeah, I am."

"But what about Nora? Wouldn't she rather stay in Seattle? What about your parents?"

He placed his hands on my shoulders. "Nora's already texted me to say she'd never forgive me if I didn't pick Farmington. And I think my parents have counted on me coming here, since this is sort of like an olive branch of sorts. They've spent the last three days on the phone with the Hadleys and are really warming up to the idea. Roger and Darlene are ecstatic at the thought of having their friends so close. As far as I know, they've already planned trips and everything. So really, the only person I need to ask is you."

"Wow. You'd be living—wow! You're serious?"

Tony nodded. "But I come with a price. You saw what happened in Seattle. I can't guarantee no one will know who I am here. It could get crazy again. Are you—could you handle that?" He bit his lip and looked so worried and adorably cute.

Laughing, I threw my arms around his waist and willed my stupid tears to stay put. "Yes!" *Come to Farmington!*

"You're sure it'll be okay? I mean, you're sure you don't have another werewolf boyfriend here you don't want me to know about?"

"Ugh! Whatever."

"Okay, just checking." He chuckled before asking, "So, where's your dad? I've met your mom, but I'm thinking it's about time I start getting to know the family. He doesn't have a shotgun, does he?"

"Nope. But I'm sure they'll make you go through the *real* Dating Ritual before we go out."

"What? The one Darlene did was fake?"

"No worries. A guy who can sing in front of thousands of people? When it comes to my mom and dad, it's in the bag."

"I'm not so sure about that. I mean, you got your orneriness from somewhere."

Ugh. "You know, you're lucky I'm really happy right now."

"So that's the secret—keep her happy and you won't get mutilated."

"Hey!"

"Done." Tony leaned in and kissed me again.

I was happy. Very, very happy.

Isn't life crazy sometimes? It's amazing the way it can throw you a whole slew of curveballs without you even realizing it. I needed a wake-up call. I needed to find out what everyone around me already knew—that reality is way better than anything I'd ever find in a book. After all, real life can be far superior. Believe me, I know!

ABOUT THE AUTHOR

♥

Jenni James is a busy mom of seven children who is married to a totally hot Air Force recruiter. When she isn't busy chasing her kids around the house, she's dreaming of new romantic books to write. *Northanger Alibi* is the second book in Jenni's series, The Jane Austen Diaries. The first book in the series, *Pride & Popularity,* was released by Inkberry Press in August 2011. The third book, *Persuaded,* will be released in summer 2012.

To find out more about The Jane Austen Diaries or Jenni's other projects, please visit her website, authorjennijames.com, or her Facebook page, Author Jenni James. She loves to hear from her readers and may be contacted at jenni@authorjennijames.com.

For a sneak peek at *Persuaded,*

the next book in The Jane Austen Diaries,

just turn the page!

PERSUADED
CHAPTER ONE

♥

I felt a twist and a slight jerk before the glass beads spilled all over the floor.

I'm such an idiot! This isn't even my necklace!

He was supposed to have left by now. He'd already said goodbye to his friends. I watched as Gregory hovered in the doorway, obviously debating what to do. I decided I'd make it easier for him. I knelt on the floor and turned my back, completely ignoring him as I started to pick up the mess.

There. Now you can go. I don't need you. I sighed at the thought of being such a klutz in front of him. Suddenly, I saw long, lean fingers close to my shorter ones, picking up beads. I glanced up at the top of Gregory's blond head as he avoided looking at me. It had been years since I'd seen that head and those hands so close to my own.

What I expected least was the joy of having him so near. I'd anticipated misery and pain and awkwardness, but never joy. Since his return, I'd fully expected him to break my heart—a punishment I deserved.

Stunned into silence by my thoughts, I began to collect the beads again. This time I looked over and noticed that not only had Gregory placed the beads he'd collected into a pile, he'd also begun to organize them into groups of color and size.

Is he stalling? My heart began to race. *Is he waiting for me to say something? He can't be hoping to be next to me longer, since he hates me. Hasn't he looked straight through me—as if I didn't exist—during the entire party? We haven't spoken one word to each other the whole night. Even when we were introduced, he just nodded and walked back to that girl.* The beautiful brunette was, even now, waiting for him in the hall.

One blue glass bead. One green glass bead. One silver spacer bead. One . . .

"Thank you, Greg–Gregory."

He looked up then, but he still didn't meet my eyes.

I tried again. "You didn't have to, but thank you anyway. It was very nice of you." *And more than I deserve.*

He raised his head quickly as if my words shocked him, and his eyes finally met mine. My heart stopped. His deep, chocolate brown eyes set against blond hair and perfect features were as striking as I remembered. He was older, three years older. *And extremely good-looking. Dang, he's hot!* my foolish heart whispered.

His eyes held mine far longer than my heart could handle, yet I didn't want to look away. I couldn't. I'd waited too long to see his incredible eyes again. Selfishly, I absorbed every moment he gave. There was so much I wish I could've said—so much I am sure he wouldn't want to hear, but I let it be. I remained silent and allowed the moment of our first real meeting in years to overwhelm me. I lived in the moment—something I was chided for doing three years ago. Something I vowed I would never make the mistake of *not* doing again. Never again would I be persuaded to disobey my heart.

He didn't smile. He didn't frown. He just searched my eyes and said, "You're welcome."

His unfamiliar deep baritone jarred me. If I wasn't frozen before, I was now. *He spoke to me. He actually spoke to me!*

I could see that he was very surprised. I realized that he must've broken some small vow to himself in that moment—probably a vow to never speak to me again.

Within seconds, he was standing again. He was going to leave, and there was nothing I could do to keep him next to me, nothing I could say. But I'd given that chance up long ago. He wasn't, nor would he ever be, mine.

His tall form towered over me, and I watched as he adjusted his jacket. And then he was gone, his eyes never once wavering from the hallway, where the beautiful girl waited for him.

In silence I collected the last pieces of the borrowed necklace I'd been so eager to wear, the necklace that had always looked so pretty on my stepsister.

Then I fled the party. I had to get away before anyone saw me freak out.

In the privacy of my car, I allowed the full force of the pain and bitterness of the last three years to wash over me. *How can I be foolish enough to love someone who I know has hated me for so long? And why did he come back? Why did he choose now—of all times—to disrupt my life? And why does he have to be so good-looking, too? I would've gladly taken him back, no matter what he looked like, but for him to be so gorgeous is torture.*

No one recognized or remembered him but me. Why would they? He was older, more muscular than he'd been at fifteen. His hair was now cut shorter and swept off his face, and his dark, rectangle-framed glasses were gone. I missed his glasses. He also introduced himself as Gregory instead of Greg.

The new, improved Gregory was cheerfully welcomed into my so-called friends' circle. Their eagerness to stake a claim at so fine a specimen reminded me of vultures circling their prey. The same girls that had gossiped about the awkward Greg and secretly mocked him, now gladly turned to Gregory with open arms.

It was rumored that his father had become very successful after leaving Farmington, New Mexico, and that Gregory's family was now worth millions. They were *millionaires,* while my family, who used to spend our winters in Hawaii and our summers in Alaska, now had to learn to economize. Thanks to the economy and the recession, our investments and businesses were deteriorating, and our finances were nearly depleted.

My dad didn't think I knew, but I had overheard him and my stepmom countless times, debating the great burden of debt that seemed to swallow us whole. Just last week, they'd announced we were going to move. My stepmom made up some pretense of having a difficult time keeping up such a large house, but I knew we didn't have a choice. At least my parents were being smart about it. We'd all be better off with a smaller house that fit within our new budget.

But why did Gregory's family have to buy our house, of all houses? That was the final blow. The house hadn't even been on the market when the realtor called to arrange a showing while I was at school Thursday. *Thank goodness I was at school!* My dad had mentioned that a tall, good-looking guy had come to the showing with his parents. I probably would have fainted had I seen him then—would've thought I was hallucinating or something. How many times in the last three years had I wished I could see Gregory? But to have my wish granted now —to see him in my house because his parents were buying it—I couldn't bear it. To have him sleeping in one of the bedrooms, or hanging out in the living room, or putting his feet up with a good book in the study—it was just too much.

"Amanda!"

I let out an involuntary shriek at the sound of my name and someone pounding on the passenger window of my car, which was still parked in front of Kylie's house. I hadn't driven away. I'd promised to help her clean up, and I would. I rolled down the window to hear her better.

"I thought you'd gone! What are you doing out here, anyway?"

I quickly put the warm beads, still clutched in my hand, into the pullout drawer beneath my stereo. "I—uh, I was just—"

"Oh, never mind," she interrupted. "You're coming in to help, aren't you?'

"Yes, of course." I hurriedly opened the car door and stepped out.

Kylie was still complaining. "Everyone else has gone already, you weirdo! What a funny thing to do. Only you would sit alone in your car at night, in the dark, when there was a party going on!"

Great, she's in a mood. I followed her silently up the steps of her house and took the large, black trash bag she handed me.

"Well, here. Since you like being in the dark anyway, I assume you won't mind cleaning up out here first." She looked at me and then shook her head before opening the front door and waltzing in. "I'll be inside. Hurry up, okay?"

"Okay," I mumbled to an already-shut door. With another sigh, I surveyed the damage from our friends. I guess it could've been worse—it was mostly cans and wrappers everywhere.

Kylie had thought it would be fun to have a piñata at the party. It was fun. But by the looks of it, most of the candy wrappers ended up outside. Relieved that I didn't have to give Gregory another thought, I started to clean up. In no time at all, I was back in the house and picking trash in there, too.

Kylie's parents had one rule when it came to throwing a party in their house. If Kylie threw a party, she had to clean it up. That meant she wasn't allowed to leave any of it for the cleaning lady who came by Monday through Saturday. I don't think Kylie had ever thrown a party where I wasn't there beforehand to help set up, and still there afterwards to help clean up.

"So, you lucky girl, tell me all about it."

"What?" I turned around. She was wearing an apron and looked positively gorgeous in it, like a model for one of those Pillsbury commercials on TV. "Tell you all about what?" I stared at her in confusion. *Did I miss something?*

"Hello? About Gregory Wentworth. Do you think I'm blind?"

Does she know? I decided to stall a bit. "Blind?" My heart began to race.

Kylie rolled her eyes. "Come on, the hottest guy here tonight totally comes to your rescue, and you can't even say anything about it?"

Oh! "Uh, yeah. He's really nice."

"Nice? You mean nice looking, right?"

"That too."

"Amanda! You were closer to him than anyone else at the party tonight. I want details, girl! Weren't you just totally freaking out? Did he say anything to you?"

"No, nothing really."

"Ugh! Only *you* would totally waste an opportunity like that. No offense, but seriously, girl, if he had helped me with my necklace, he would've had my phone number by the time he stood up. I don't care who he came with!"

I smiled weakly. Her words hurt more than I think she'd intended them to.

"Did he say who that girl was? I heard from someone that she was from Bloomfield."

"No, he didn't say anything." I leaned over and tossed a soda can in the trash bag.

"Well, I'll just have to find out who she is."

I glanced up just as Kylie flipped her hair and folded her arms. The look on her face spoke volumes.

I was worried. "Are you going to break them up or something?"

"First, let's see if they're going out. I don't want to do something drastic if I don't have to."

I lowered my eyes a minute before smiling bravely. "So, you think he'll go for you? Do you think he likes you?"

"If he doesn't, yet, I promise you, he will."

I nodded my head. *She's right. I mean, what guy could resist Kylie Russell? What guy would* want *to?*

"Can you believe it? Gregory's a multi-millionaire! And he's moving here, of all places." She laughed. "To think I thought this summer was going to be boring!"

I attempted a chuckle. *This summer? This summer will most likely prove to be painful. Horrible. Awkward. But it won't be boring.*

STAY IN TOUCH WITH JENNI JAMES

****

Visit authorjennijames.com

to learn more about Jenni,

read interviews and reviews,

and get all the details on upcoming titles.

****

Become a fan on facebook

Author Jenni James

The Jane Austen Diaries

Follow me on twitter Jenni_james

Send me an email jenni@authorjennijames.com